SLADE HOUSE

SLADE HOUSE
David Mitchell

Alfred A. Knopf Canada

PUBLISHED BY ALFRED A. KNOPF CANADA

Copyright © 2015 David Mitchell
Illustrations © 2015 Neal Murren

www.penguinrandomhouse.ca

Alfred A. Knopf Canada and colophon are registered trademarks.

Library and Archives Canada Cataloguing in Publication

Mitchell, David (David Stephen), author
Slade House / David Mitchell.

Issued in print and electronic formats.

ISBN 978-0-345-81019-9
eBook ISBN 978-0-345-81021-2

I. Title.

PR6063.I785S63 2015   823'.92   C2015-902403-X

Jacket image: Paper sculpture © Jeff Nishinaka

Printed and bound in the United States of America

10 9 8 7 6 5 4 3 2 1

Penguin
Random House
KNOPF CANADA

THE
RIGHT
SORT

1979

Whatever Mum's saying's drowned out by the grimy roar of the bus pulling away, revealing a pub called The Fox and Hounds. The sign shows three beagles cornering a fox. They're about to pounce and rip it apart. A street sign underneath says WESTWOOD ROAD. Lords and ladies are supposed to be rich, so I was expecting swimming pools and Lamborghinis, but Westwood Road looks pretty normal to me. Normal brick houses, detached or semi-detached, with little front gardens and normal cars. The damp sky's the colour of old hankies. Seven magpies fly by. Seven's good. Mum's face is inches away from mine, though I'm not sure if that's an angry face or a worried one. 'Nathan? Are you even listening?' Mum's wearing make-up today. That shade of lipstick's called Morning Lilac but it smells more like Pritt Stick than lilacs. Mum's face hasn't gone away, so I say, 'What?'

'It's "Pardon" or "Excuse me". Not "What?"'

'Okay,' I say, which often does the trick.

Not today. 'Did you hear what I told you?'

'"It's 'Pardon' or 'Excuse me'. Not 'What?'"'

3

'Before that! I said, if anyone at Lady Grayer's asks how we came here, you're to tell them we arrived by taxi.'

'I thought lying was wrong.'

'There's lying,' says Mum, fishing out the envelope she wrote the directions on from her handbag, 'which *is* wrong, and there's creating the right impression, which is necessary. If your father paid what he's supposed to pay, we really would have arrived by taxi. Now . . .' Mum squints at her writing. 'Slade Alley leads off Westwood Road, about halfway down . . .' She checks her watch. 'Right, it's ten to three, and we're due at three. Chop chop. Don't dawdle.' Off Mum walks.

I follow, not stepping on any of the cracks. Sometimes I have to guess where the cracks are because the pavement's mushy with fallen leaves. At one point I had to step out of the way of a man with huge fists jogging by in a black and orange tracksuit. Wolverhampton Wanderers play in black and orange. Shining berries hang from a mountain ash. I'd like to count them, but the *clip-clop-clip-clop* of Mum's heels pulls me on. She bought the shoes at John Lewis's sale with the last of the money the Royal College of Music paid her, even though British Telecom sent a final reminder to pay the telephone bill. She's wearing her dark blue concert outfit and her hair up with the silver fox-head hairpin. Her dad brought it back from Hong Kong after World War Two. When Mum's teaching a student and I have to make myself scarce, I sometimes go to Mum's dressing table and get the fox out. He's got jade eyes and on some days he smiles, on others he doesn't. I don't feel well knitted today, but the Valium should kick in soon. Valium's great. I took two pills. I'll have to miss a few next week, so Mum won't notice her supply's going down. My tweed jacket's scratchy. Mum got it from Oxfam specially for today, and the bow tie's from Oxfam, too. Mum volunteers there on Mondays so she can get the best of the stuff people bring in on Saturdays. If Gaz Ingram or anyone in his gang sees me in this bow tie, I'll find a poo in my locker, guaranteed. Mum says I have to learn how to Blend In more, but there aren't any classes for Blending In, not even on the town library noticeboard. There's a Dungeons & Dragons club advertised there, and I always want to go, but Mum says I can't because Dungeons & Dragons is playing with dark forces. Through one front window I see horse racing. That's *Grandstand* on BBC1. The next three windows have net curtains, but then I see a TV with wrestling on it. That's Giant Haystacks the hairy baddie fighting Big Daddy the bald goodie on ITV. Eight houses later I see *Godzilla* on BBC2. He knocks down a pylon just by blundering into it and a Japanese fireman with a sweaty face is shouting into a radio. Now Godzilla's picked up a train, which makes no sense because amphibians don't have thumbs. Maybe Godzilla's thumb's like a panda's so-called thumb, which is really an evolved claw. Maybe—

'Nathan!' Mum's got my wrist. 'What did I say about dawdling?'

I check back. '"Chop chop!"; "Don't dawdle".'

'So what are you doing now?'

'Thinking about Godzilla's thumbs.'

Mum shuts her eyes. 'Lady Grayer has invited me – us – to a musical gathering. A soirée. There'll be people who care about music there. People from the Arts Council, people who award jobs, grants.' Mum's eyes have tiny red veins like rivers photographed from very high up. 'I'd rather you were at home playing with your Battle of the Boers landscape too, but Lady Grayer insisted you come along, so . . . you *have* to act normal. Can you do that? Please? Think of the most normal boy in your class, and do what he'd do.'

Acting Normal's like Blending In. 'I'll try. But it's not the Battle of the Boers, it's the Boer War. Your ring's digging into my wrist.'

Mum lets go of my wrist. That's better.

I don't know what her face is saying.

Slade Alley's the narrowest alley I've ever seen. It slices between two houses, then vanishes left after thirty paces or so. I can imagine a tramp living there in a cardboard box, but not a lord and lady.

'No doubt there'll be a proper entrance on the far side,' says Mum. 'Slade House is only the Grayers' town residence. Their proper home's in Cambridgeshire.'

If I had 50p for every time Mum's told me that, I'd

now have £3.50. It's cold and clammy in the alley like White Scar Cave in the Yorkshire Dales. Dad took me when I was ten. I find a dead cat lying on the ground at the first corner. It's grey like dust on the moon. I know it's dead because it's as still as a dropped bag, and because big flies are drinking from its eyes. How did it die? There's no bullet wound or fang marks, though its head's at a slumped angle so maybe it was strangled by a cat-strangler. It goes straight into the Top Five of the Most Beautiful Things I've Ever Seen. Maybe there's a tribe in Papua New Guinea who think the droning of flies is music. Maybe I'd fit in with them. 'Come along, Nathan.' Mum's tugging my sleeve.

I ask, 'Shouldn't it have a funeral? Like Gran did?'

'No. Cats aren't human beings. Come along.'

'Shouldn't we tell its owner it won't be coming home?'

'How? Pick it up and go along Westwood Road knocking on all the doors saying, "Excuse me, is this your cat?"'

Mum sometimes has good ideas. 'It'd take a bit of time, but—'

'*Forget* it, Nathan – we're due at Lady Grayer's right now.'

'But if we don't bury it, crows'll peck out its eyes.'

'We don't have a spade or a garden round here.'

'Lady Grayer should have a spade and a garden.'

Mum closes her eyes again. Maybe she's got a headache. 'This conversation is over.' She pulls me away and we go down the middle section of Slade Alley. It's about five houses long, I'd guess, but hemmed in by brick walls so high you can't see anything. Just sky. 'Keep your eyes peeled for a small black iron door,' says Mum, 'set into the right-hand wall.' But we walk all the way to the next corner, and it's ninety-six paces exactly, and thistles and dandelions grow out of cracks, but there's no door. After the right turn we go another twenty paces until we're out on the street parallel to Westwood Road. A sign says CRANBURY AVENUE. Parked opposite's a St John ambulance. Someone's written CLEAN ME in the dirt above the back wheel. The driver's got a broken nose and he's speaking into a radio. A mod drives past on a scooter like off *Quadrophenia*, riding without a helmet. 'Riding without a helmet's against the law,' I say.

'Makes no sense,' says Mum, staring at the envelope.

'Unless you're a Sikh with a turban. Then the police'll—'

'"A small black iron door": I mean . . . how did we miss it?'

I know. For me, Valium's like Asterix's magic potion, but it makes Mum dopey. She called me Frank yesterday – Dad's name – and didn't notice. She gets two prescriptions for Valium from two doctors because one's not enough, but—

—a dog barks just inches away and I've shouted and jumped back in panic and peed myself a bit, but it's okay, it's okay, there's a fence, and it's only a small yappy dog, it's not a bull mastiff, it's not *that* bull mastiff, and it was only a bit of pee. Still, my heart's hammering like mad and I feel like I might puke. Mum's gone out into Cranbury Avenue to look for big gates to a big house, and hasn't even noticed the yappy dog. A bald man in overalls walks up, carrying a bucket and a pair of stepladders over his shoulder. He's whistling 'I'd Like to Teach the World to Sing (in Perfect Harmony)'.

Mum cuts in. 'Excuse me, do you know Slade House?'

The whistling and the man stop. 'Do I know What House?'

'Slade House. It's Lady Norah Grayer's residence.'

'No idea, but if you find Her Ladyship, tell her I fancy a bit o' posh if she fancies a bit o' rough.' He tells me, 'Love the dickie bow, son,' and turns into Slade Alley, picking up his whistling where he left off. Mum looks at his back, muttering, 'Thanks a heap for bloody nothing.'

'I thought we weren't supposed to say "bloody"—'

'Don't start, Nathan. Just – don't.'

I think that's Mum's angry face. 'Okay.'

The dog's stopped yapping to lick its willy. 'We'll backtrack,' Mum decides. 'Maybe Lady Grayer meant the next alley along.' She goes back into Slade Alley and I follow. We reach the middle section in time to see the stepladder man vanish around the corner of the far end, where the moon-grey cat's still lying dead. 'If someone killed you down here,' I remark, 'nobody'd see.' Mum ignores me. Maybe it wasn't very Normal. We're halfway down the middle bit when Mum stops: 'I'll be *jiggered*!' There's a

9

small black iron door, set into the brick wall. It's small all right. I'm four feet eleven inches, and it's only up to my eyes. A fat person'd need to squeeze hard to get through. It has no handle, keyhole, or gaps around the edges. It's black, nothing-black, like the gaps between stars. 'How on earth did we miss that?' says Mum. 'Some Boy Scout *you* are.'

'I'm not in the Scouts any more,' I remind her. Mr Moody our scoutmaster told me to get lost, so I did, and it took the Snowdonia mountain rescue service two days to find my shelter. I'd been on the local news and everything. Everyone was angry, but I was only following orders.

Mum pushes the door, but it stays shut. 'How on earth does the bally thing open? Perhaps we ought to knock.'

The door pulls my palm up against it. It's warm.

And as it swings inwards, the hinges shriek like brakes . . .

. . . and we're looking into a garden; a buzzing, still summery garden. The garden's got roses, toothy sunflowers, spatters of poppies, clumps of foxgloves, and lots of flowers I can't name. There's a rockery, a pond, bees grazing and butterflies. It's epic. 'Cop a load of *that*,' says Mum. Slade House is up at the top, old, blocky, stern and grey and half smothered by fiery ivy, and not at all like the houses on Westwood Road and Cranbury Avenue. If it was owned by the National Trust they'd charge you £2 to get in, or 75p for children under sixteen. Mum and I have already stepped in through the small black iron door, which the wind closed like an unseen butler, and currents are pulling us up the garden, around by the wall. 'The Grayers must have a full-time gardener,' says Mum, 'or even several of them.' At last, I feel my Valium kicking in. Reds are glossier, blues glassier, greens steamier and whites see-through like one layer of a two-ply tissue. I'm about to ask Mum how such a big house and its garden can possibly fit in the space between Slade Alley and Cranbury Avenue, but my question falls down a deep well with no bottom, and I forget what I've forgotten.

'Mrs Bishop and son, I presume,' says an invisible boy. Mum jumps, a bit like me with the yappy dog, but now my Valium's acting like a shock absorber. 'Up here,' says the voice. Mum and me look up. Sitting on the wall, about fifteen feet up I'd say, is a boy who looks my age. He's got wavy hair, pouty lips, milky skin, blue jeans, pumps but no socks and a white T-shirt. Not an inch of tweed, and no bow tie. Mum never said anything about other boys at Lady Grayer's musical soirée. Other boys mean questions have to get settled. Who's coolest? Who's hardest? Who's brainiest? Normal boys care about this stuff and kids like Gaz Ingram fight about it. Mum's saying, 'Yes, hello, I'm Mrs Bishop and this is Nathan – look, that wall's jolly high, you know. Don't you think you ought to come down?'

'Good to meet you, Nathan,' says the boy.

'Why?' I ask the soles of the boy's pumps.

Mum's hissing something about manners and the boy says, 'Just because. I'm Jonah, by the way. Your welcoming committee.'

I don't know any Jonahs. It's a maroon-coloured name.

Mum asks, 'And is Lady Norah your mother, Jonah?'

Jonah considers this. 'Let's say she is, yes.'

'Right,' says Mum, 'that's, um, I see. Do—'

'Oh, splendid, Rita, you've found us!' A woman walks out from a lattice-frame tunnel thing. The tunnel's smothered with bunches of dangly white and purple flowers. The woman's around Mum's age, but she's slim and less worn down and dresses like her garden looks. 'After I hung up last night, I rather got the collywobbles that I'd horribly confused you by giving you directions to the Slade Alley door – really, I should've sent you round the front. But I did so want your first sight of Slade House to be across the garden in its full splendour.'

'Lady Grayer!' Mum sounds like an imitation of a posh person. 'Good afternoon. No no no, your directions were—'

'Call me Norah, Rita, *do* – the whole "Lady" thing's a frightful bore when I'm off duty. You've met Jonah, I see: our resident Spider-Man.' Lady Grayer has Jonah's black hair and X-ray vision eyes that I prefer to look away from.

'*This* young man must be Nathan.' She shakes my hand. Her hand's pudgy but its grip's strong. 'Your mother's told me all about you.'

'Pleased to meet you, Norah,' I say, like a grown-up from a film.

'Nathan!' says Mum, too loud. 'Lady Grayer didn't mean *you* can call her by her Christian name.'

'It's fine,' says Norah Grayer. 'Really, he's welcome to.'

The bright afternoon sways a bit. 'Your dress matches the garden,' I say.

'What an elegant compliment,' says Lady Grayer. 'Thank you. And you look very smart, too. Bow ties are terribly distinguished.'

I extract my hand. 'Did you own a moon-grey cat, Norah?'

'"Did" I own a cat? Do you mean recently, or in my girlhood?'

'Today. It's in the alley.' I point in the right direction. 'At the first corner. It's dead.'

'Nathan can be rather direct sometimes.' Mum's voice is odd and hurried. 'Norah, if the cat is yours, I'm terribly—'

'Don't worry, Slade House has been catless for some years. I'll telephone our odd-job man and ask him to give the poor creature a decent burial pronto. That's most thoughtful of you, Nathan. Like your mother. Have you inherited her musical gift, too?'

'Nathan doesn't practise enough,' says Mum.

'I practise an hour a day,' I say.

'Ought to be two,' says Mum, crisply.

'I've got homework to do too,' I point out.

'Well, "Genius *is* nine parts perspiration",' says Jonah, standing right behind us, on the ground – Mum gasps with surprise, but I'm impressed. I ask, 'How did you get down so quickly?'

He taps his temple. 'Cranially implanted teleport circuitry.'

I know he jumped really, but I like his answer better. Jonah's taller than me, but most kids are. Last week Gaz Ingram changed my official nickname from Gaylord Baconface to Poison Dwarf.

'An incurable show-off,' sighs Norah Grayer. 'Now, Rita, I do hope you won't mind, but Yehudi Menuhin's dropped by and I told him about your Debussy recital. He's positively bursting to meet you.'

Mum makes a face like an astonished kid from *Peanuts*: '*The* Yehudi Menuhin? He's here? This afternoon?'

Lady Grayer nods like it's no big deal. 'Yes, he had a "gig" at the Royal Festival Hall last night, and Slade House has become his London bolt-hole-cum-pied-à-terre, as it were. Say you don't mind?'

'*Mind*?' says Mum. 'Meeting Sir Yehudi? Of course I don't mind, I just . . . can't quite believe I'm awake.'

'*Bravissima.*' Lady Grayer takes Mum by the arm and steers her towards the big house. 'Don't be shy – Yehudi's a teddy bear. Why don't you chaps' – she turns to Jonah and me – 'amuse yourselves in this glorious sunshine for a little while? Mrs Polanski's making coffee éclairs, so be sure to work up an appetite.'

'Eat a damson, Nathan,' says Jonah, handing me a fruit from the tree. He sits down at the base of one tree, so I sit down against its neighbour.

'Thanks.' Its warm slushy flesh tastes of early August mornings. 'Is Yehudi Menuhin really visiting?'

Jonah gives me a look I don't understand. 'Why on earth would Norah lie?'

I've never met a boy who calls his mum by her Christian name. Dad'd call it 'very modern'. 'I didn't say she *is* lying. It's just that he's an incredibly famous virtuoso violinist.'

Jonah spits his damson stone into tall pink daisies. 'Even incredibly famous virtuoso violinists need friends. So how old are you, Nathan? Thirteen?'

'Bang on.' I spit my stone farther. 'You?'

'Same,' he says. 'My birthday's in October.'

'February.' I'm older, if shorter. 'What school do you go to?'

'School and I never saw eye to eye,' says Jonah. 'So to speak.'

I don't understand. 'You're a kid. You have to go. It's the law.'

'The law and I never got on, either. 'Nother damson?'

'Thanks. But what about the truancy officer?'

Jonah's face may mean he's puzzled. Mrs Marconi and me have been working on 'puzzled'. 'The what officer?'

I don't get it. He must know. 'Are you taking the piss?'

Jonah says, 'I wouldn't dream of taking your piss. What would I do with it?' That's kind of witty, but if I ever used it on Gaz Ingram he'd crucify me on the rugby posts. 'Seriously, I'm taught at home.'

'That must be *ace*. Who teaches you? Your mum?'

Jonah says, 'Our master,' and looks at me.

His eyes hurt, so I look away. Master's like a posh word for 'teacher'. 'What's he like?'

Jonah says, not like he's trying to boast, 'A true genius.'

'I'm dead jealous,' I admit. 'I hate my school. *Hate* it.'

'If you don't fit into the system, the system makes life hell. Is your father a pianist too, like your mother?'

I like talking about Dad as much as I hate talking about school. 'No. Dad lives in Salisbury but Salisbury in Rhodesia, not Wiltshire. Dad's from there, from Rhodesia, and he works as a trainer for the Rhodesian Army. Lots of kids tell fibs about their dads, but I'm not. My dad's an ace marksman. He can put a bullet between a man's eyes at a hundred metres. He let me watch him once.'

'He let you watch him put a bullet between a man's eyes?'

'It was a shop dummy at a rifle range near Aldershot. It had a rainbow wig and an Adolf Hitler moustache.'

Doves or pigeons coo in the damson trees. No one's ever very sure if doves and pigeons are the same bird or not.

'Must be tough,' says Jonah, 'your father being so far away.'

I shrug. Mum told me to keep shtum about the divorce.

'Have you ever visited Africa?' asks Jonah.

'No, but Dad promised I can visit next Christmas. I was meant to go last Christmas, but Dad suddenly had lots of soldiers to train. When it's winter here, it's summer there.' I'm about to tell Jonah about the safari Dad's going to take me on, but Mrs Marconi says talking's like ping-pong: you take turns. 'What job does your dad do?'

I'm expecting Jonah to tell me his father's an admiral or a judge or something lordly, but no. 'Father died. Shot. It was an accident on a pheasant shoot. It all happened a long, long time ago.'

Can't be that *long ago*, I think, but I just say, 'Right.'

The purple foxgloves sway like something's there . . .

. . . but there isn't, and Jonah says, 'Tell me about your recurring nightmare, Nathan.' We're sitting by the pond on warm paving slabs. The pond's a long rectangle, with water lilies and a bronze statue of Neptune in the middle gone turquoise and bruised. The pond's bigger than our whole garden, which is really just a muddy yard with a washing line and rubbish bins. Dad's lodge in Rhodesia has land going down to a river where there're hippos. I think of Mrs Marconi telling me to 'Focus on the *subject*'. 'How do you know about my nightmare?'

'You have that hunted look,' says Jonah.

I lob a pebble up, high over the water. Its arc is maths.

'Is your nightmare anything to do with your scars?'

Immediately my hand's pulled my hair down over the white-and-pink-streaked area below my right ear, to hide where the damage shows the most. The stone goes *plop!* but the splash is invisible. I won't think about the mastiff launching itself at me, its fangs pulling skin off my cheek like roast chicken, its eyes as it shook me like a doll, its teeth locked around my jawbone; or the weeks in hospital, the injections, the drugs, the surgery, the faces people make; or how the mastiff's still waiting for me when I fall asleep.

A dragonfly settles on a bulrush an inch from my nose. Its wings are like cellophane and Jonah says, 'Its wings are like cellophane,' and I say, 'I was just thinking that,' but Jonah says, 'Just thinking what?' so maybe I just thought he'd said it. Valium rubs out speech marks and pops thought-bubbles. I've noticed it before.

In the house, Mum's playing warm-up arpeggios.

The dragonfly's gone. 'Do you have nightmares?' I ask.

'I have nightmares,' says Jonah, 'about running out of food.'

'Go to bed with a packet of digestives,' I tell him.

Jonah's teeth are perfect, like the smiley kid with zero fillings off the Colgate advert. 'Not that kind of food, Nathan.'

'What other kinds of food are there?' I ask.

A skylark's Morse-coding from a far far far far star.

'Food that makes you hungrier, the more of it you eat,' says Jonah.

Shrubs tremble blurrily like they're being sketched in.

'No wonder you don't go to a normal school,' I say.

Jonah winds a stem of grass around his thumb . . .

. . . and snaps it. The pond's gone and we're under a tree, so obviously it's another stem of grass, a later snap. The Valium's throbbing in my fingertips now, and the sunlight's a harpist. Fallen leaves on the shaved lawn are shaped like tiny fans. 'This tree's a ginkgo tree,' says Jonah. 'Whoever lived at Slade House half a century ago planted it.' I start arranging ginkgo leaves into a large Africa, about one foot from Cairo to Johannesburg. Jonah's lying on his back now, either asleep or just with his eyes closed. He hasn't asked me about football once, or said I'm gay for liking classical music. Maybe this is like having a friend. Time must've passed, because my Africa's finished. I don't know the time exactly because last Sunday I took my watch apart to improve it, and when I put it back together again some pieces were missing. Not quite like Humpty Dumpty. Mum cried when she saw the watch's insides and shut herself in her room so I had to eat cornflakes for tea again. I don't know why she got upset. The watch was old, dead old, made long before I was

19

even born. The leaves I remove for Lake Victoria, I use for Madagascar.

'Wow,' says Jonah, leaning his head on an elbow.

Do you say 'Thanks' when someone says 'Wow'? I don't know so I play safe and ask 'Do you ever think you might be a different species of human, knitted out of raw DNA in a laboratory like in *The Island of Doctor Moreau*, and then turned loose to see if you can pass yourself off as normal or not?'

Gentle applause flutters down from an upstairs room.

'My sister and I *are* a different species,' says Jonah, 'but the experiment part is redundant. We pass ourselves off as normal, or anything we want to be. Do you want to play fox and hounds?'

'We walked past a pub called The Fox and Hounds.'

'It's been there since the 1930s. Smells like the 1930s too, if you ever go in. My sister and I borrowed its name for a game. Want to play? It's a race, basically.'

'I didn't know you had a sister.'

'Don't worry, you'll meet her later. Fox and hounds is a race. We start off at opposite corners of the house. We both shout, "Fox and hounds, one two three!" and on the "three" we start running, anti-clockwise, until one of us catches the other. The catcher is the hound and the one who's caught is the fox. Simple. Up for it?'

If I say no to Jonah he might call me a wuss or a spazzo. 'Okay. But shouldn't it be called "fox and *hound*" if there's only one hound?'

Jonah's face goes through two or three expressions I can't read. 'Henceforth, Nathan, it'll be known as "fox and hound".'

Slade House looms up. The red ivy's redder than red ivy normally is. The ground floor windows are too high off the ground to see inside, and anyway they only reflect the sky and clouds. 'You stay here,' Jonah tells me at the front right corner. 'I'll go round the back. Once we start, run anti-clockwise – up this way.' Off Jonah trots down the side of the house, which is walled by a holly hedge. While I'm waiting, I notice someone moving in the window nearest to me. I step closer, peering up. It's a woman. Another guest at Lady Norah Grayer's soirée, I suppose, or maybe a servant. She's got one of those beehive hairstyles that ladies on Dad's old LPs had; her forehead's furrowed and her mouth's slowly opening and closing like a goldfish. Like she's repeating the same word over and over and over. I can't hear what she's saying because the window's shut, so I tell her, 'I can't hear you.' I take a step forwards, but she vanishes and there's only reflected sky. So I take a step back, and she's there again. It's like one of those pictures you get in cereal boxes where it looks like the image is moving when you tilt it slightly. The beehive woman could be saying, 'No, no, no'; or 'Go, go, go'; or it might be 'Oh, oh, oh'. Before I work it out, I hear Jonah's voice down the holly path, saying, 'Ready, Nathan?'

I shout, 'Ready!' and when I look back at the window the beehive woman's gone, and I can't get her back wherever I stand or however I tilt my head. I take up my starting position at the corner.

'Fox and hound!' calls Jonah, and I call it too. 'One, two—'

'*Three!*' I shout back and leg it down the holly path – *slap slap slap* go my shoes, and the echo's *whack whack whack*. Jonah's taller than me and maybe he'd beat me over a hundred metres, but I could still end up as the hound and not the fox because it's stamina that counts over longer distances, and I'm at the end of the side path already, where I was expecting a view of Cranbury Avenue, but there's just a long brick wall and fir trees and a narrow strip of lawn that goes by in a blur. I pound along and swing round on a drainpipe, sprint down another chilly side path sliced with blades of light coming through a high fence with brambles poking between the slats, then I'm out front again where I smack into a butterfly bush and butterflies blizzard up all orange and black and red and white and one goes in my mouth so I spit it out and I leap over the rockery and nearly trip up when I land but I don't. Along I run past steps climbing to the front door, past the beehive woman's window but she's gone now and then round the corner and I'm pounding back down the echoey holly path, starting to get a stitch in my side but I'll ignore it, and the holly's scratching the back of my hand like it's pushing in, and I wonder if Jonah's gaining on me or I'm gaining on Jonah but not for long because I'm back at the back of Slade House, where the fir trees are thicker and bigger and the wall blurrier, and I keep running running running round the corner to where the brambles really are choking through the fence now, scratching my shins my neck and now I'm afraid I'll be the fox not the hound, and round the front the sun's gone in, or gone out, or gone away, and the flowers are withered and there's not a single butterfly on the butterfly bush, just dead ones smeared into the path, powder-paint skid marks with one half-dead one, flapping a bit . . .

I've stopped, because the far end of the garden, the wall with the small black door – it's gone all faint and dim. Not because of evening. It can't even be four o'clock yet. Not because it's misty, either. I look up – the sky's still bluish, like it was before. It's the garden itself. The garden's fading away.

I turn round to tell Jonah to stop the game, something's wrong, we need a grown-up. Any second now he'll come hurtling round the far corner. The brambles sway like underwater tentacles. I glance back at the garden. There was a sundial but it's gone now, and the damson trees too. Am I going blind? I want Dad to tell me it's fine, I'm not going blind, but Dad's in Rhodesia, so I want Mum. Where's Jonah? What if this dissolving's got him too? Now the lattice tunnel thing's erased. What do you do when you're visiting someone's house and their garden starts vanishing? The blankness is moving closer like a storm front. Then, at the far end of the brambly side path, Jonah appears, and I relax for a second because he'll know what to do, but as I watch, the running-boy shape gets fuzzier and becomes a growling darkness with darker eyes, eyes that know me, and fangs that'll finish what they started and it's pounding after me in sickening slow motion, big as a cantering horse and I'd scream if I could but I can't my chest's full of molten panic it's choking me choking it's wolves it's winter it's bones it's cartilage skin liver lungs it's Hunger it's Hunger it's Hunger and *Run!* I run towards the steps of Slade House my feet slipping on the pebbles like in dreams but if I fall it'll have me, and I've only got moments left and I stumble up the steps and grip the doorknob *turn please turn* it's stuck no no no it's scratched gold it's stiff it's ridged does it turn yes no yes no twist pull push pull turn twist I'm falling forwards onto a scratchy doormat on black and white tiles and my shriek's like a shriek shrieked into a cardboard box all stifled and muted—

'What on earth's the matter, Nathan?' I'm on my banged knees on a carpet in a hallway, my heart's going *slap slap slap slap slap slap* but it's slowing, it's slowing, I'm safe, and Lady Grayer's standing right here holding a tray with a little iron teapot on it with vapour snaking up from the spout. 'Are you unwell? Shall I fetch your mother?'

Woozily, I get up. 'Something's outside, Norah.'

'I'm not sure I understand. What kind of a something?'

'I mean, a, a, a . . . kind of . . .' A kind of what? 'Dog.'

'Oh, that's Izzy, from next door. Daft as a brush, and she *will* insist on doing her business in the herb garden. It's jolly annoying, but then she's very sweet.'

'No, it was a . . . bigger . . . and the garden was vanishing.'

Lady Norah Grayer does a smile, though I'm not sure why. '*Fab*ulous to see boys using their imaginations! Jonah's cousins kneel before the TV with their Atari thingummies, their bleepy-bleepy space games, and I tell them, "It's a beautiful day! Play outside!" and they say, "Yeah, yeah, Auntie Norah, if you say so."'

The hallway has black and white tiles like a chessboard. I smell coffee, polish, cigar smoke and lilies. Through a little diamond-shaped window in the door, I peer out and see the garden. It's not at all dissolved. Down the far end, I can see the small black iron door onto Slade Alley. I must have imagined too hard. Down the stairs comes Tchaikovsky's 'Chant de l'alouette'. It's Mum.

Norah Grayer asks, 'Nathan, are you feeling all right?'

I looked up Valium in a medical encyclopedia at the library and in rare cases it can make you hallucinate and you have to tell your doctor immediately. I guess I'm rare. 'Yes, thanks,' I say. 'Jonah and me were playing fox and hound and I think I got carried away.'

'I *thought* you and Jonah might have a rapport – and golly gosh, Yehudi and your mother are getting on like a house on fire! You go on up to the soirée, up both these flights of stairs. I'll find Jonah, and we'll bring the éclairs. Up you go now. Don't be shy.'

I take off my shoes and put them side by side and climb the first flight of stairs. The walls are panelled and the stair carpet's thick as snow and beige like nougat. Up ahead, there's a little landing where a grandfather clock's going *krunk . . . kronk . . . krunk . . . kronk . . .* but first I pass a portrait of a girl, younger than me, plastered with freckles, and wearing a pinafore thing from Victorian times. She's dead lifelike. The banister glides under my fingertips. Mum plays the last note of 'Chant de l'alouette' and I hear applause. Applause makes her happy. When she's sad, it's only crackers and bananas for dinner. The next portrait's of a bushy-browed man in a regimental uniform: the Royal Fusiliers. I know because Dad got me a book about British Army regiments and I memorised it. *Krunk . . . kronk . . . krunk . . . kronk* goes the clock. The last portrait before the landing is a pinched lady in a hat who looks a lot like Mrs Stone, our RE teacher. If Mrs Marconi asked me to guess, I'd say this hat lady was wishing she was anywhere but here. From the little landing, another flight of stairs to my right carries on up to a pale door. The clock's really tall. I put my ear against its wooden chest and hear its heart: *krunk . . . kronk . . . krunk . . . kronk . . .* It has no hands. It's got words instead, on its old, pale-as-bone clock face, saying TIME IS and under that TIME WAS and under that TIME IS NOT. Up the second flight of steps, the next picture's of a man who's twenty or so, with slick black hair and squinty eyes and a look like he's unwrapped a present and can't work out what it is. The last-but-one portrait's a lady I recognise. It's the hair. The lady I saw in the window. Same dangly earrings, too, but a dreamy smile instead of streaky eyeshadow. She must be a friend of the Grayers. Look at that mauve vein in her neck, it's throbbing, and a murmur's in my ear saying, *Run now, as fast as you can, the way you came in . . .* and I say, 'What?' and the voice stops. Was it even there? It's Valium. Maybe I shouldn't take any more for a while. Only a few steps to the pale door now, and I hear Mum's voice on the other side: 'Oh no, Yehudi, you mustn't make me hog the lime-light when there's so much talent in the room!' The reply is too soft to hear, but people laugh. Mum, too. When did I last hear Mum laugh like that? 'You're all too kind,' I hear her say. 'How could I say no?' Then she starts up 'Danseuses de Delphes'. I take two or three steps and draw level with the last portrait.

Which is me.

Me, Nathan Bishop . . .

Wearing exactly what I'm wearing now. This tweed jacket. This bow tie. Only in the picture I've got no eyes.

..at's my big nose, the zit on my chin I've had all week, my scarring from the mastiff under my ear, but no eyes. A joke? Is this funny? I never know. Mum must've sent a school photograph plus photographs of the clothes I was going to be wearing to Norah Grayer, and she got the artist to paint this. How else? This isn't bad Valium, is it? Is it? I blink hard at the portrait, then kick the skirting board; not hard enough to break my toe, but hard enough to hurt. When I don't wake up, I know I'm awake. The clock's going *krunk-kronk-krunk-kronk* and I'm trembling with anger. I know anger when I feel it. Anger's an easy one, it's like being a boiling kettle. Why did Mum play a joke on me on a day she told me to Act Normal? Normally I'd wait until Debussy was over before opening the pale door but Mum doesn't deserve manners today so I put my hand on the doorknob.

I sit up in bed. What bed? Not my bed in my titchy room in England, that's for sure: this is three times the size, with sunlight blasting through the curtains and Luke Skywalker on the sheet-thing. My head's humming. My mouth's dry. There's a desk; a bookshelf full of *National Geographics*; strings of beads over the doorway; a million insects outside; a Zulu-style tribal shield and spear decorated with tinsel that brings the answer closer now, closer, closer . . .

Dad's lodge in the Bushveld. I let out this bark of relief and all my dream-anger at Mum goes *phffft*. It's Christmas

Eve, and I'm in Rhodesia! Yesterday I flew here on a British Airways flight, all on my own, my very first time on a plane, and asked for the fish pie because I didn't know what boeuf bourguignon was. Dad and Joy met me at the airport in his jeep. On the way here we saw zebras and giraffes. No spooky portraits, no Slade House, no mastiff. Mrs Todds my English teacher gives an automatic *F* if anyone ever writes 'I woke up and it was all a dream' at the end of a story. She says it violates the deal between reader and writer, that it's a cop-out, it's the Boy Who Cried Wolf. But every single morning we really do wake up and it really was all a dream. It's a shame Jonah's not real, though. I lift up the curtain by my bed and see slopes of woodland and grassland, going on forever. Down below's the brown river where there're hippos. Dad sent me a Polaroid of this exact view. It's on my wall at home in England by my pillow, but here it's the actual view. African birds, African morning, African birdsong. I smell bacon and get up. I'm in my Kays Catalogue pyjamas. The pine floor's knotty, warm and grooved on the soles of my feet, and the strings of beads are like lots of fingertips on my face . . .

Dad's at the table, reading his *Rhodesian Reporter* and dressed in his short-sleeved khaki shirt. 'The Kraken wakes.' Dad always says that in the mornings. It's the title of a book by John Wyndham about a monster who melts the ice caps and floods the world.

I sit down. 'Morning, Dad.'

Dad folds his newspaper. 'Well, *I* wanted to wake you for your first African dawn, but Joy said, "No, let the poor lad sleep in, he flew twelve hours non-stop." So we'll do all that tomorrow. Hungry?' I nod – I guess I must be – and Dad tilts his head at the kitchen hatch: 'Joy? Violet? Young man needs his chow!'

The hatch opens and Joy appears. 'Nathan!' I knew about Joy, who Mum calls 'your father's dolly bird', but it was still a jolt to see Dad holding hands with another woman. They're going to have a baby in June, so they must've had sexual intercourse. The baby'll be my half-brother or half-sister, but it hasn't got a name yet. I wonder what it does all day. 'Sleep well?' says Joy. Joy's got a Rhodesian accent like Dad's.

'Yes. Mad dreams, though.'

'I *always* have mad dreams after a long-haul flight. OJ, bacon sandwich do you, Nathan?'

I like how Joy says 'OJ'. Mum would hate it. 'Yes please.'

'He'll need some coffee, too,' says Dad.

'Mum says I'm too young for caffeinated drinks,' I say.

'Horse pucky,' says Dad. 'Coffee's the elixir of life, and Rhodesian coffee's the purest on Earth. You're having some.'

'OJ, bacon sandwich *and* coffee, coming up,' says Joy. 'I'll get Violet on it straight away.' The hatch closes. Violet's the maid. Mum often used to shout at Dad, 'I'm not your bloody maid, you know, Frank!' Dad lights his pipe, and the smell of his tobacco brings back memories of when he and Mum were married. He says from the corner of his mouth, 'Tell me about this dream of yours, matey.'

The gazelle's head's distracting, and so are Dad's grand-father's muskets from the Boer War and the ceiling fan. 'Mum took me to see a lady, like a lord-and-lady-type lady. The house was missing so we asked a sort of window cleaner man but he didn't know either . . . then we found it, it was this big house like in *To the Manor Born*. There was a boy called Jonah but he turned into a big dog. Yehudi Menuhin was there too, and Mum played with him upstairs' – Dad snorts a laugh – 'and then I saw a portrait of me, but my eyes were missing, and . . .' I see a small black iron door in the corner. 'That door was there, too.'

Dad looks round. 'Dreams do that. Mix reality with moonshine. You were asking about my gun-room door before you turned in last night. Don't you remember?'

I must've, if Dad says so. 'It all felt so real when I was in it.'

'I know it *felt* real, but you can see it wasn't. Right?' I look at Dad's brown eyes, crinkly lines, tanned skin, greyish streaks in his sandy hair, his nose like mine. A clock's going *krunk . . . kronk . . . krunk . . . kronk . . .* and there's a trumpeting noise outside, not far away. I look at Dad, hoping it is what I think it is. 'Dead right, matey: a herd drifted across the river yesterday afternoon. We'll go see 'em later, but first, line your stomach.'

31

'Here we go,' says Joy, placing a tray in front of me. 'Your first African breakfast.' My bacon sandwich looks epic, with a triple layer of rashers, and ketchup dribbling out.

'That's God's own bacon sarnie,' I say. Someone said that line on a sitcom I saw once and lots of people laughed.

'Well aren't *you* the charmer?' says Joy. 'Wonder who you get *that* from . . .'

Dad puts his arm around Joy's waist. 'Try the coffee first. It'll make a man of you.' I lift the mug and peer down. Inside's black as oil, as holes in space, as Bibles.

'Violet ground the beans just now,' says Joy.

'God's own coffee,' says Dad. 'Drink up now, matey.'

Some stupid part of me says, *No, don't, you mustn't.*

'Your mother'll never know,' says Dad. 'Our little secret.'

The mug's so wide it covers my nose like a gas mask. The mug's so wide it covers my eyes, my whole head. Then whatever's in there starts gulping me down.

Time passed, but I don't know how much. A slit of light opens its eye and becomes a long flame. Cold bright star white. A candle, on a candlestick, on the scarred floorboards. The candlestick's dull silver or pewter or lead and it's got symbols on it, or maybe letters from a dead language. The flame's not moving, it's as if time's unspooled and jammed. Three faces hang in the gloom. Lady Grayer on my left, but she's younger now, younger than Mum. To my right is Jonah Grayer but he's older than the Jonah in the garden. They're twins, I think. They're wearing grey cloaks with hoods half down; his hair's short and hers is long, and it's gold instead of black like before; and they're kneeling like they're praying, or meditating. They're still as waxworks. If they're breathing, I can't see it. The third face is Nathan Bishop's, opposite me. I'm a reflection in a mirror, a tall rectangle, standing on the floor. I'm still wearing the tweed jacket from Oxfam, and the bow tie. When I try to move, I can't. Not a muscle. I can't turn my head, or lift my hand, or speak, or blink, even. Like I've been paralysed. It's scary as hell, but I can't even go *Mmmfff* like scared gagged people do. I'm pretty sure this can't be heaven or hell, but I know it's not Rhodesia. Dad's lodge was a kind of vision. I'd pray it's only the Valium making me see this, but I don't believe in God. I'm in an attic, judging from the sloping ceiling and rafters. Are the Grayers prisoners like me? They look like the Midwich Cuckoos. Where's Yehudi Menuhin, all the guests, the soirée? Where's my mum?

The flame comes to life, and the symbols on the candlestick change, and keep changing as if it's thinking fast and the symbols are its thoughts. Jonah Grayer's head shifts. His clothes rustle. 'Your mother sends her apologies,' he says, touching his face as if he's testing whether it still fits. 'She had to leave.' I try to ask 'Why? Where?' but nothing I need to speak – jaw, tongue, lips – works. Why would

Mum leave without me? The me in the mirror gazes back. Neither of us can move. Norah Grayer's flexing her fingers like she's just waking up. Did they inject me with something? 'Every time I come back to my body,' she says, 'it feels less of a homecoming, and more like entering an alien shell. A more enfeebled one. Do you know, I want to be free of it?'

'Be careful what you wish for,' says Jonah. 'If anything happened to your birth-body, your soul would dissolve like a sugar cube and—'

'I know perfectly well what would happen.' Norah Grayer's voice is chillier and throatier now. 'The hairdresser paid an uninvited visit, I saw.'

Jonah asks, 'What hairdresser are you talking about?'

'Our previous guest. Your "Honey Pie". She appeared in a window. Then on the stairs, by her portrait, she tried to give some sort of a warning to the boy.'

'Her afterimage showed up in a window, you mean. It happens. The girl is gone, as gone as a smoke ring puffed out years ago in a gale off Rockall. It's harmless.'

A brownish moth fusses around the candle flame.

'They're getting bolder,' says Norah Grayer. 'The time will come when a "harmless afterimage" will sabotage an Open Day.'

'If – if – our Theatre of the Mind were ever "sabotaged" and a guest escaped, we'd simply call our friends the Blackwatermen to bring them back again. That's why we pay them. Handsomely.'

'You underestimate ordinary people, Jonah. You always did.'

'Would it kill you, Sister, to once, just *once*, say, "Top job, a superb orison, you've landed us a juicy, tenderised soul to pay the power bills for the next nine years – *bon appetit!*"?'

'Your African lodge could not have been a cornier ersatz mishmash, Brother, if Tarzan had swung in on a vine.'

'It wasn't sup*posed* to be real; it only had to match the Bushveld the guest *imag*ined. Anyway, the boy's mentally abnormal. He hasn't even noticed his lungs have stopped working.' Jonah now looks at me like Gaz Ingram does.

It's true. I'm not breathing. My switched-off body hasn't raised the alarm. I don't want to die. *I don't want to die.*

'Oh stop snivelling, for Christ's sake,' groans Jonah. 'I cannot abide snivellers. Your father would be ashamed of you. Why, *I* never snivelled when I was your age.'

'"Never snivelled"?' snorts Norah. 'When Mother died—'

'Let's reminisce later, Sister. Dinner is served. It's warm, confused, afraid, it's imbibed banjax, and it's ready for filleting.'

The Grayer twins make letters in the air with their hands. There's a slow thickening in the dark, above the candle, at a little above head height. The thickening becomes a something. Something fleshy, lumpish, fist-size, pulsing blood red, wine red, blood red, wine red, faster and brighter, the size of a human head, but more like a heart as big as a football, just suspended there. Veins grow out of it, like jellyfish tentacles, and twist like ivy through the air. They're coming for me. I can't turn my head or even shut my eyes. Some of the vein-things finger their way into my mouth, others into my ears, two up my nostrils. When I see my reflection, I'd scream if I could, or pass out, but I can't. Then a dot of pain opens up on my forehead.

In the mirror, there's a black spot there. Something . . .

. . . oozes out, and hovers there inches from my eyes, look: a clear cloud of stars, small enough to fit in your cupped palms. My soul.

Look.

Look.

Beautiful as, as . . .

Beautiful.

The Grayer twins lean in, their faces shining like Christmas, and I know what they're hungry for. They pucker up their lips and suck. The round cloud stretches doughily into two smaller round clouds . . . and splits. One half of my soul goes into Jonah's mouth, and the other into Norah's. They shut their eyes like Mum did the time we saw Vladimir Ashkenazy at the Royal Albert Hall. Bliss. *Bliss*. Inside my skull, I howl and my howl echoes on and on and on and on but nothing lasts forever . . . The big beating heart-thing's gone, and the Grayer twins are back kneeling where they were before. Time's slowed down to nothing. The flame's stopped flickering. The brownish moth is frozen an inch away from it. Cold bright star white. The Nathan in the mirror's gone, and if he's gone, I'm—

SHINING
ARMOUR

1988

'*Good evening, here are today's headlines at six o'clock on Saturday, October the twenty-second. Speaking at a press conference in Downing Street today, the Home Secretary, Douglas Hurd, rejected criticism of the government's ban on broadcast interviews with members of the Irish Republican party, Sinn Féin. Mr Hurd said—*' I switched off the radio, got out of my car and looked up at the pub. The Fox and Hounds. A memory came back to me, of me and Julie popping in for a drink here one time. We were house-hunting, and we'd viewed a place on Cranbury Avenue, one street up. It'd sounded all right in the estate agent's but a right bloody shithole it turned out to be – damp, gloomy, with a garden too small to bury a corpse in, it was so depressing we needed a liquid pick-me-up just to face the drive home. Five years ago, that was. Five years, one wedding, one dismal honeymoon in Venice, four Christmases with Julie's god-awful pinko, tree-hugging relatives, fifteen hundred bowls of Shredded Wheat, two hundred and fifty bottles of wine, thirty haircuts, three toasters, three cats, two promotions, one Vauxhall Astra, a few boxes of Durex, two emergency visits to the dentist, dozens of arguments of assorted sizes and one beefed-up assault charge later, Julie's still living in our cottage with a view of woods and horses, and I'm in a flat behind the multistorey car park. Mr Justice Jones said I was lucky I wasn't booted out of the force. Thank God me and Julie'd never had kids, otherwise she'd be shafting me for child support as well as compensation for her 'disfigurement'. Grasping bitch. Five years gone. Blink of a bloody eye.

I set off down Westwood Road, eyes peeled. I asked a woman in a miniskirt and ratty fake fur coat — on the game, I'd bet a tenner — if she'd heard of Slade Alley, but she shook her head and strode by without stopping. A jogger ran past in a blur of orange and black but joggers are tossers. Three Asian kids went trundling past on skateboards, but I'd had enough of our curry-munching cousins for one day so I didn't ask them. The multi-culty brigade bleat on about racism in the force, but I'd like to see them keep order in a town full of Everywherestanis whose only two words of English are 'police' and 'harassment', and whose alleged women walk about in tall black tents. There's more to public order than holding hands and singing 'Ebony and Ivory'.

The streetlights came on and it was looking like it might rain: the sort of weather that used to give Julie her mysterious headaches. I was tired after a long and stressful day and at the 'sod this for a game of soldiers' stage, and if our chief super was anyone but Trevor Doolan I'd have buggered off home to the remains of last night's tandoori takeaway, had a laugh at the Sharons and Waynes on *Blind Date*, then seen if Gonzo and a few of the lads were up for a pint. Unfortunately Trevor Doolan *is* our chief super and a walking bloody lie detector to boot, and come Monday he'd be asking me some rectal probe of a question that I'd only be able to answer if I'd really followed up Famous Fred Pink's 'lead'. It'd be 'Describe this alley to me, then, Edmonds . . .' or some such. With my appraisal in November and the Malik Enquiry due to report in two weeks, my tongue has to stay firmly up Doolan's arse. So down Westwood Road I trogged, looking left, looking right, searching high and low for Slade Alley. Could it have been blocked off since Fred Pink's day, I wondered, and the land given to the house-owners? The Council sometimes do that, with our blessing; alleyways are trouble spots. I got to the end of the road where the A2 skims past a park and dropped my fag down a gutter. A guy with a busted nose was sat behind the wheel of a St John ambulance and I nearly asked him if he knew Slade Alley, but then I thought, *Bugger it*, and headed back towards my car. Maybe a swift beer at The Fox and Hounds, I thought. Exorcise Julie's ghost.

About halfway back down Westwood Road I happened upon an altercation between a five-foot-nothing traffic warden and two brick shithouses at least eighteen inches taller, wearing fluorescent yellow jackets and with their backs to me. Builders, I could just bloody tell. None of the trio noticed me strolling up behind them. 'Then your little notebook's *wrong*.' Builder One was prodding the traffic warden on the knot of his tie. 'We weren't here until *after* four, gettit?'

'I was 'ere,' wheezed the traffic warden, who was the spit of that Lech Wałęsa, that Polish leader, but with an even droopier moustache. 'My watch—'

'Your little watch is telling you porkies,' said Builder Two.

The traffic warden was turning pink. 'My watch is accurate.'

'I hope you're a good performer in court,' said Builder One, ''cause if there's one thing juries hate more than traffic wardens, it's *short*, little Napoleon, privatised traffic wardens.'

'My height's nothing to do with illegal flamin' parking!'

'Ooh, the F-word!' said Builder Two. 'Verbal abuse, that is. And he didn't call me "sir" once. You're a disgrace to your clip-on tie.'

The traffic warden scribbled on his ticket book, tore off the page and clipped it under the wiper of a dirty white van they were standing next to. 'You've got fourteen days to pay or face prosecution.'

Builder One snatched the parking ticket off the windscreen, wiped it on his arse and scrumpled it up.

'Very tough,' said Lech Wałęsa, 'but you'll still have to pay.'

'Will we? 'Cause we both heard you ask for a bribe. Didn't we?'

Builder Two folded his arms. 'He asked for fifty quid. I could hardly believe my ears. Could you believe your ears?'

The traffic warden's jaw worked up and down: 'I did not!'

'Two against one. Mud sticks, my faggoty friend. Think about your little pension. Do the clever thing, turn round, and go—'

'What *I* just heard was conspiracy to bear false witness,' I said, and both builders swivelled round, 'and to pervert the course of justice.' The older of the two had a broken nose and a shaved head. The younger one was a freckled carrot-top with raisin eyes too close together. He spat out some chewing gum onto the pavement between us. 'Plus litter offences,' I added.

The Broken Nose stepped up and peered down. 'And you are?'

Now I'm not one to boast, but I cut my teeth in the Brixton riots and earned a commendation for bravery at the Battle of Orgreave. It takes more than a hairy plasterer to put the shits up me. 'Detective Inspector Gordon Edmonds, CID, Thames Valley Police.' I flashed my ID. 'Here's a suggestion. Pick up that ticket *and* that gum; climb into your pile-of-shit van; go; and pay that fine on Monday. That way I might not bring a tax audit down on you on Tuesday. What's that face for? Don't you like my fucking language? *Sir?*'

★

Me and the traffic warden watched them drive off. I lit up a smoke and offered one to Lech Wałęsa, but he shook his head. 'No, thanks all the same. My wife would murder me. I've given up. Apparently.'

Pussy-whipped: no surprise. 'Bit of a thankless job, huh?'

He put away his pad. 'Yours, mine or being married?'

'Ours.' I'd meant his. 'Serving the Great British Public.'

He shrugged. 'At least you get to put the boot in sometimes.'

'*Moi*? Poster boy for community policing, me.'

A Bob Marley lookalike walked straight at us. The traffic warden stood to one side, but I didn't. The Dreadlocked Wonder missed me by a provocative centimetre. The traffic warden glanced at his watch. 'Just happened to be passing, Detective Inspector?'

'Yes and no,' I told him. 'I'm looking for an alleyway called Slade Alley, but I'm not sure it even exists. Do you know it?'

Lech Wałęsa gave me a look that started off puzzled; then he smiled, stepped aside and did a flourish like a crap magician to reveal a narrow alleyway cutting between two houses. It turned left at a corner twenty yards away, under a feeble lamp mounted high up.

'This is it?' I asked.

'Yep. Look, there's the sign.' He pointed at the side of the right-hand house where, sure enough, a smeary old street sign read SLADE ALLEY.

'Shag me,' I said. 'Must've walked straight past it.'

'Well, y'know. One good turn deserves another. Better be off now – no rest for the wicked, and all that. See you around, Officer.'

Inside the alley, the air was colder than out on the street. I walked down to the first corner, where the alley turned left and ran for maybe fifty paces before turning right. From up above, Slade Alley'd look like half a swastika. High walls ran along the entire length, with no overlooking windows. Talk about a mugger's paradise. I walked down the middle section, just so I'd be able to look Chief Super Doolan in his beady eye and tell him I inspected every foot of Slade Alley, sir, and found doodly bloody squat, sir. Which is why I came across the small black iron door, about halfway down the middle section on the right. It was invisible till you were on top of it. It only came up to my throat and was about two feet wide. Now, like most people, I'm many things – a West Ham supporter, a Swampy from the Isle of Sheppey, a freshly divorced single man, a credit-card debtor owing my Flexible Friend over £2,000 and counting – but I'm also a copper, and as a copper I can't see a door opening onto a public thoroughfare without checking if it's locked. Specially when it's getting dark. The door had no handle but when my palm pressed the metal, lo and behold the bloody thing just swung open easy as you please. So I stooped down a bit to peer through . . .

★

. . . and where I'd expected a shitty little yard, I found this long garden with terraces and steps and trees, all the way up to a big house. Sure, the garden'd gone to seed a bit, with weeds and brambles and stuff, and the pond and shrubbery'd seen better days, but it was pretty breathtaking even so. There were roses still blooming, and the big high wall around the garden must've sheltered the fruit trees because they still had most of their leaves. And Jesus Christ, the house . . . A real mansion, it was. Grander than all the other houses around, half covered with red ivy. Big tall windows, steps going up to the front door, the lot. The curtains were drawn, but the house sort of glowed like vanilla fudge in the last of the evening light. Just beautiful. Must be worth a bloody mint, specially with the housing market going through the roof right now. So why oh why oh why had the owners left the garden door open for any Tom Dick or Harry to amble in and do the place over? They must be bloody mental. No burglar alarm either, so far as I could see. That really got my goat – 'cause guess who gets the job of picking up the pieces when the houses of the rich get broken into? The boys in blue. So I found myself walking up the stony path to give the owner a talking-to about domestic security.

My hand was on the knocker when a soft quiet voice said, 'Can I help you?' and I turned round to find this woman at the foot of the steps. She was about my age, blonde, with bumps in all the right places under a man's baggy granddad shirt and gardening trousers. Quite a looker, even in her wellies.

'Detective Inspector Edmonds, Thames Valley Police.' I walked down the steps. 'Good evening. Are you the owner of this property, madam?'

'Yes, I - I'm Chloe Chetwynd.' She held out her hand the way some women do, fingers together and knuckles upwards, so it's hard to shake properly. I noticed her wedding ring. 'How can I help you, Detective . . . uh, oh God, forgive me, your name – it came and went.'

'Edmonds, Mrs Chetwynd. Detective Inspector.'

'Of course, I . . .' Chloe Chetwynd's hand fluttered near her head. Then she asked the standard question: 'Has anything happened?'

'Not yet, Mrs Chetwynd, no; but unless you get a lock on that garden gate, something will happen. I could have been anyone. Think about it.'

'Oh gosh, the gate!' Chloe Chetwynd pushed a strand of waxy gold hair off her face. 'It had a, a sort of . . . wire clasp thing, but it rusted away, and I meant to do something about it, but my husband died in June, and everything's been a bit . . . messy.'

That explains a lot. 'Right, well, I'm sorry to hear about your loss, but a burglar'd leave your life one *hell* of a lot messier. Who else lives here with you, Mrs Chetwynd?'

'Just me, Detective. My sister stayed on for a fortnight after Stuart died, but she has family in King's Lynn. And my cleaner comes in twice a week, but that's all. Me, the mice and the things that go bump in the night.' She did a nervous little smile that wasn't really a smile.

Tall purple flowers swayed. 'Do you have a dog?'

'No. I find dogs rather . . . slavish?'

'Slavish or not, they're better security than a "wire clasp thing". I'd get a triple mortice lock fitted top, middle and bottom, with a steel frame. People forget a door's only as tough as its frame. It'll cost you a bit, but a burglary'll cost you more.'

'A "triple mortar lock"?' Chloe Chetwynd chewed her lip.

Jesus Christ the rich are bloody hopeless. 'Look, down at the station we use a contractor. He's from Newcastle-upon-Tyne so you'll only catch one word in five, but he owes me a favour. Chances are he'll drop by in the morning if I give him a bell tonight. Would you like me to call him?'

Chloe Chetwynd did a big dramatic sigh. 'Gosh, would you? I'd be so grateful. DIY was never my forte, alas.'

Before I could reply, footsteps came pounding down the side of the house. Two kids were about to appear, running at full pelt, and I even stepped onto the lowest step to give them a clear run . . .

. . . but the footsteps just faded away. Must've been kids next door and some acoustic trick. Chloe Chetwynd was giving me an odd look, however. 'Did you hear them?'

'Sure I did. Neighbours' children, right?'

She looked unsure and nothing made sense for a moment. Her grief must have turned her into a bag of nerves. Inheriting a big old tomb of a house can't have helped. I regretted not handling her a bit more gently earlier, and gave her my card. 'Look, Mrs Chetwynd, this is my direct line, in case of . . . anything.'

She gave my card the once-over, then slipped it into her gardening trousers. Against her thigh. 'That's extremely kind. I – I feel safer already.'

The red ivy shivered. 'Grief's a bastard, it really is – pardon my French. It makes everything else harder.' I couldn't decide what colour Chloe Chetwynd's eyes were. Blue. Grey. Lonely as hell.

The woman asked, 'Whom did you lose, Detective?'

'My mum. Leukaemia. A long time ago.'

'There's no such thing as "a long time ago".'

I felt all examined. 'Did your husband die in an accident?'

'Pancreatic cancer. Stuart lived longer than the doctors predicted, but . . . in the end, you know . . .' The evening sun lit the softest fuzz on her upper lip. She swallowed, hard, and looked at her wrist as if there was a watch there, though there wasn't. 'Gosh, look at the time. I've detained you long enough, Detective. May I walk you back to the offending door?'

We walked under a tree that'd shed lots of little leaves shaped like fans. I plucked a waist-high weed from the side of the lawn. 'Golly gosh,' sighed Mrs Chetwynd, 'I've let this poor garden go to rack and ruin, haven't I?'

'Nothing a little elbow grease couldn't put right.'

'I'll need industrial quantities of the stuff to tame this jungle, alas.'

'I'm surprised you don't employ a gardener,' I said.

'We did, a Polish chap, but after Stuart died he left to pursue other career opportunities. With a brand-new Flymo.'

I asked, 'Did you report the theft?'

She looked at her nails. 'I just couldn't face the kerfuffle. There was so much else to see to. Pathetic of me, really, but . . .'

'I only wish I'd known. So I could've helped.'

'That's sweet of you.' We passed under a trellissy thing with purple and white flowers hanging down. 'If it's not nosy of me,' she asks, 'were you in Slade Alley on police business when you found the door? Or were you just passing through, by chance?'

Famous Fred Pink'd slipped my mind the moment I set foot in the garden. 'Police business, as it happens.'

'Gosh. Nothing majorly unpleasant, I hope.'

'Majorly pointless, I suspect — unless the names Norah Grayer or Rita and Nathan Bishop mean anything to you, on the off chance?'

She frowned: 'Norah Grayer . . . no. Odd name. Are the Bishops that husband and wife team who present the breakfast show on ITV?'

'No,' I replied. 'Not to worry. It's a bit of a saga.'

We'd come to the end of the stony path but instead of showing me out, Chloe Chetwynd sat down on a low wall by a sundial. 'My frantic social calendar just happens to be empty this evening,' she said, a bit foxily, 'if you're in the mood for telling me the saga, Detective.'

Why hurry back to my poky flat? I got my smokes out of my leather jacket. 'May I? And would you?'

'Yes, you may; and yes, I would. Thank you.'

So I joined her on the low wall, lit one for her, one for me. 'Okay, Part One. Rita and Nathan Bishop were a mother and son who lived over near the station, and who disappeared in 1979. Enquiries were made at the time, but when the investigating officer found out that Rita Bishop was up to her eyeballs in debt and had relatives in Vancouver, it was assumed she'd skipped town, and the case died from lack of interest.' A light breeze blew the woman's cigarette smoke into my face, but I didn't mind. 'On to Part Two. Six weeks ago, a man named Fred Pink woke up in the coma ward of the Royal Berkshire Hospital.'

'Now *him* I do know,' said Chloe Chetwynd. 'He was in the *Mail on Sunday*: "The Window Cleaner Who Came Back from the Dead".'

'One and the same.' I tapped ash onto the top of the wall where a few ants were crawling around. 'When not enjoying his fifteen minutes of fame, Fred Pink was down the town library, catching up on the local papers. Which is where he came across an article about the Bishops' disappearance – and lo and behold, he recognised them. Or thinks he did. Says he even spoke with Rita Bishop, the mum, out there –' I nod at the small black iron door

'– in Slade Alley, around three o'clock, October twenty-seventh, 1979. A Saturday.'

Chloe Chetwynd looked politely astonished. 'That's precise.'

'It was an unforgettable day for him, you see. After Rita Bishop had asked him if he knew where "Norah Grayer's residence" was, Fred Pink lugged his ladder out of Slade Alley onto Westwood Road, where a speeding taxi knocked him into his nine-year coma.'

'What a story!' Chloe Chetwynd sort of sloughs off her wellies to let her feet breathe. 'But if this Norah Grayer character really is minor gentry, she shouldn't be so very difficult to track down.'

I made a gesture of agreement. 'You'd think so, but our searches so far have only drawn blanks. Assuming she exists.'

Chloe Chetwynd inhaled, held the smoke in her lungs, and breathed out. 'Well, if she *did* exist, and *did* live around here, she'd probably live in Slade House – our house. Mine, that is. But Stuart and I bought the house from people called Pitt, not Grayer, and they'd lived here for years.'

'Since before 1979?' I asked.

'Since before the war, I believe. And as for me, in 1979 I was a history of art postgrad living in Luxembourg and finishing a thesis on Ruskin. Of course, Detective, you're more than welcome to bring in the sniffer dogs, or dredge the pond, if you think there's anything sinister on the property . . .'

A squirrel darted across the clumpy lawn and vanished

into a rhubarb patch. I wondered who the hell Ruskin was. 'I don't think that'll be necessary, Mrs Chetwynd. After everything Fred Pink's been through, my chief super thought we should do him the courtesy of following up his lead, but to be honest, strictly between you and me, we're not really expecting anything much to come of it.'

Chloe Chetwynd nodded. 'That's decent of you, to show Mr Pink you're taking him seriously. And I *do* hope that the Bishops are alive and well somewhere.'

'If I were a betting man, I'd put a sizeable chunk on them being alive, well and solvent somewhere in British Columbia.' The moon was above the chimneys and TV aerials. My imagination opened one side of its dirty mac and showed me a picture of Chloe Chetwynd squirming on her back, under me. 'Well, I really ought to be off. I'll tell the contractor to come round the main entrance, shall I?'

'Whichever suits.' She stood and walked me the last few steps to the small black iron door. I drummed my fingers on it, wondering whether to go for her phone number, but Chloe Chetwynd then said this: '*Mrs* Edmonds made a wise choice of husband, Detective.'

Oho? 'That area of my life's a bloody train wreck, Mrs Chetwynd. I'm dumped, single, with the bruises to prove it.'

'All the best TV detectives have complex domestic lives. And really, address me as Chloe, if that's allowed.'

'Off duty, it's allowed. Off duty, I'm Gordon.'

Chloe toyed with a button on the cuff of her granddad shirt. 'That's settled, then, Gordon. *Au revoir.*'

I stooped and sort of posted myself through the ridiculously small doorway to get back into Slade Alley. We shook hands over the threshold. Over Chloe's shoulder I thought I saw movement and a blink of light in an upper window of Slade House, but I probably didn't. I thought of my flat, of the washing-up in the sink, of the leaking radiator, of the copy of *Playboy* stashed behind my toilet brush, and wished I was inside Slade House now, looking over the twilit garden, knowing Chloe'd soon be coming back, cream-skinned under her clothes. 'Get yourself a cat,' I heard myself say.

She smiled and frowned at the same time: 'A cat?'

Back on Westwood Road, the cars all had their headlights and wipers on, and raindrops splashed my neck and my not-quite-yet-bald spot. My visit to Chloe Chetwynd hadn't been conducted exactly as per standard police protocol, I had to admit. I'd lowered my guard, we'd sort of flirted at the end, and Trevor Doolan would be most unchuffed if he'd heard me discuss Fred Pink the way I did; but now and then you meet a woman who makes you do that. It's okay, Chloe Chetwynd can keep a secret, I can tell. Julie was a blabbermouth – brash on the outside, emotional jelly on the inside – but Chloe's the reverse. Chloe's got this chipped outer shell but an indestructible core. That bit at the end when she smiled, or half smiled . . . Like when the lights come on at the end of a power cut and you think, *Hallelujah!* The way we sat down and smoked like it was the most natural thing in the world. Sure, Chloe Chetwynd has a few bob tucked away and her house is worth a fortune, and I don't have a pot to piss in, but all she's got in her life now are spiders, mice and memories of a sick husband. I may be an idiot in some respects but when it comes to women, I'm more experienced than most guys. I've slept with twenty-two women, from Angie Pike the Sheerness Bike to last month's Surrey stockbroker's bored housewife with a thing about handcuffs, and I could tell Chloe Chetwynd was thinking about me like I was thinking of her. As I walked back to my car, I felt fit and slim and strong and good and confident that something had just begun.

'*Good evening, here are today's headlines at six o'clock on Saturday, October the twenty-ninth. Earlier today, US Secretary of State George Schultz announced at a press conference in the White House that the American embassy in Moscow is to be entirely rebuilt, following the discovery of listening devices in the walls of the building. President Reagan expressed his—*' Who gives a shit, honestly? I turn off the radio, get out and lock my car. Same space as seven days ago, smack bang outside The Fox and Hounds. What a god-awful day. This morning a piss-head on speed attacked the desk sergeant just as I was passing and it took four of us to drag him to the cell — where the stupid bastard died an hour later. The toxicology

55

report'll clear us, eventually, but we're already under the Spotlight of Shame courtesy of the Malik Enquiry – whose initial findings, we found out at lunchtime, have been leaked to the bloody *Guardian*. Force Ten Fucking Shit Storm Ahoy. Doolan said he'd 'do his best' to shield me from the flak. 'Do his best'? How half-assed does *that* sound? To add yet more grit to the Vaseline, a final demand for payment from Dad's care home arrived before I left for work, along with a final *final* demand from the credit card company. I'll have to extend my overdraft, come Monday. Or try to. The one ray of sunshine to brighten up this nightmare of a day was Chloe Chetwynd calling this afternoon. She sounded nervous at first, but I told her I'd been thinking about her since last Saturday. She said she'd been thinking about me, too – and at least two of my organs went *Yes!* So after leaving the office I got myself a twenty-quid haircut at a poofter parlour and drove here via Texaco, where they sell carnations and condoms. Be prepared and all that, right? I hurry along the pavement, whistling 'When You Wish Upon a Star', swerving to avoid first a jogger in black and dayglo orange running togs, then a guy my age trundling a push-chair along. The brat's screaming blue bloody murder and the guy's face is saying, *Why oh why oh why did I shoot my wad into an ovulating female?* Too late now, pal.

There's no sign of the traffic warden at the mouth of Slade Alley tonight. Into the cold alley I go, down to the corner, turn left, onwards twenty paces, and here we are again: one small black iron door. I give it a hefty shove but tonight it stays shut. No rattle, no give, no nothing. A new frame, concreted in, with freshly laid brickwork along the bottom edge. Nice work. You couldn't even jimmy in a crowbar. I set off down towards the Cranbury Avenue end of the alley to find the main entrance to Slade House, but I'm stopped by a click and a thunk from the door behind me. Here she is, stepping out through the munchkin-size doorway: 'Good evening, Detective Inspector.' She's wearing an Aztecky poncho thing over thigh-hugging black jeans, and holding something against her breasts. I come back, peer closer and see a small ginger cat. ''Ello 'ello 'ello,' I say. 'What's all this, then?'

'Gordon, Bergerac. Bergerac, Gordon.'

'"Bergerac"? As in Jim Bergerac, the TV detective?'

'Don't say it so incredulously. Getting a cat was your idea, so it seemed appropriate. He's too cute to be a Columbo, too hairy for a Kojak, too male for Cagney or Lacey, so I settled on Bergerac. Isn't he a*dor*able?'

I look at the furry bundle. I look at Chloe's eyes. 'Totally.'

'And how about my new improved door, Gordon: will it deter unwelcome visitors, do you think?'

'Unless they're packing knee-high anti-tank missiles, yes. You can sleep safe in your bed from now on.'

A little silver shell dangles on a black cord around Chloe Chetwynd's neck. 'Look, it's so kind of you to drop by. After I put the phone down I got in a tizzy about wasting police time.'

'This isn't police time. It's my time. I'll spend it how I like.'

Chloe Chetwynd holds Bergerac against her soft throat. I smell lavender and smoke and I get that off-road feeling you get when anything's possible. She's had her hair done, too. 'In *that* case, Gordon, if I'm not pushing my luck, would you mind inspecting the door from the garden side, too? Just to ensure that my state-of-the-art triple mortice lock meets industry standards . . .'

Chloe lowers the sizzling side of beef onto her kitchen table. I sniff it in, filling my head with the gorgeous salty, greasy aroma of dead cow. The table's old and massive, as is the kitchen. Julie used to drool over pictures of kitchens like this in that magazine she got, *Country Living*. Oak beams, terracotta tiles, recessed spotlights, a view of the sloping garden, fancy blinds, a Welsh dresser with a collection of teapots, a cooker big enough to roast a small child, a Swedish stainless-steel fridge-freezer as vast as they have in American films and a built-in dishwasher. There's a fireplace with a big copper hood over it. 'You carve the meat,' says Chloe. 'That's the man's job.'

I get to work with the knife. 'This beef smells incredible.'

She brings over the roast veg. 'My mother's recipe: red wine, rosemary, mint, nutmeg, cinnamon, soy, plus a few secret ingredients that I can't reveal or I'd have to kill you.' Chloe removes the lid: parsnips, spuds, carrots, cubes of pumpkin. 'Spiced beef needs a wine with a bit of oomph. How about a punchy, dry Rioja?'

I make an *It's fine by me if it's fine with you* face.

'Rioja it is, then. I'm perr*ritty* sure I still have a Tempranillo '81 stashed away.' When Julie spoke about wine she sounded like a beautician with no O levels aping a wine buff, which is what she was. Chloe sounds like she's stating facts. She comes back and hands me the bottle and a corkscrew. With a glint in her eye? I twist the pointy bit into the cork and think carnal thoughts until the cork goes *Pop!* 'I love that sound,' says Chloe. 'Don't you? Wine Nazis say that you let these heavy reds breathe for a quarter of an hour, but I say life's too short. Here, use these glasses . . .' Their crystal bases trundle over the wood. 'Pour away, Jeeves.'

I obey. The wine goes *glug–glug–glugglugglugglug*.

The tiramisu is a stunner, and I say so. Chloe dabs at a fleck of cream on her lip with her napkin. 'Not too cloying, not too sweet?'

'Like everything else you've fed me, it was perfection. When did you find time to train as a chef?'

Looking pleased, she sips her wine and dabs away the red stain with her napkin. 'Flatterer.'

'Flattery? What motive could I *possibly* have for flattering you? None. There. Case dismissed.'

Chloe pours coffee from a pot shaped like a dragon. 'Next time – well, I mean, *if* you ever want to help me out with my over-catering again – I'll do you my vodka sorbet. Tonight, I didn't—'

Right here, right next to us, a girl calls out, *'Jonah!'*
Clear as a bell. But there's no girl here. But –
– I heard her. Right here. A girl. She said, *'Jonah!'*
There's a clattery noise from the door –
I jump, my chair scrapes, tips and falls over.
The catflap's swinging. It squeaks. It's quiet.
Then I hear the girl again: *'Jonah?'*
I didn't imagine that.
Again: *'Jooo-naaah!'*

I'm standing in a fight-or-flight crouch, but Chloe's not looking shocked, and not looking like I'm a nutcase either. She's watching me, calm and cool. My legs are trembling. I ask her, 'Did you hear that?' My voice is a bit manic.

'Yes.' If anything, she looks relieved. 'Yes, I did.'

'A girl,' I check, 'right here, in the kitchen.'

Chloe shuts her eyes and nods, slowly.

'But . . . but you said you didn't have children.'

Chloe breathes in, breathes out. 'They're not mine.'

Which is clear as mud. Adopted? *Invisible?* 'Who are they?'

'Her name's Norah. She's Jonah's sister. They live here.'

The hairs on my arms are standing up. 'I . . . You . . . *What?*'

Chloe takes one of my cigarettes. 'You hear a voice; there's no one here; it's a very old house. Any thoughts, Detective?'

I can't say the word 'ghost' – but I just heard what I just heard: a girl saying 'Jonah' when there's no girl here.

'Those footsteps you heard last Saturday,' Chloe goes on, 'round the house. You thought they were kids next door. Remember?'

I'm cold. I nod once.

'There are no kids living next door, Gordon. That was Norah and Jonah. I think they're twins. Here. Smoke. Sit down.'

I do as she says, but my mind's reeling and my fingers are clumsy as I light my cigarette.

'I first noticed them back in January, this year. In the garden, at first, like you did; and like you, I assumed it was neighbours. Then one afternoon when Stuart was flat out and asleep after chemo – Valentine's Day, as it happens – I was on the stairs when I heard a girl humming on the little landing, by the grandfather clock. But there was nobody there. Then a boy's voice called up from the doorway, *'Norah, your boiled egg's ready!'* And the girl said, *'I'll be down as soon as I've wound up the clock!'* I thought – or hoped, perhaps – they were kids who'd got in somehow, for a lark, for a dare, but . . . I was *there*, on the stairs, for heaven's sake. By the clock.'

It hasn't escaped my attention that Norah the invisible girl has the same name as Lady Grayer, but what this might mean, or whether it's a meaningless coincidence, who knows? 'Did your husband hear them?'

Chloe shakes her head. 'Never. Around Easter, Jonah and Norah – the "ghosts" – walked right through the kitchen, chattering away about a pony called Blackjack, and Stuart was sitting right where you are. He didn't even look up from his crossword. I asked, "Did you hear that?" and he replied, "Hear what?" "Those voices," I said. Stuart gave me a weird and worried look so I pretended I might've left a radio on upstairs.' Chloe lights her cigarette and gazes at the glowing tip. 'Stuart was a biochemist, an atheist, and he just didn't do ghosts. A few weeks later we had a dinner party here, and as I served up the starters I heard Jonah and Norah walk right by, singing, "*Here comes the bride, a million miles wide*" and giggling like drains. Loud as real children. We had eight guests sitting around the table, but not one of them heard.'

In the fireplace the flames snap. My CID brain telexes in the word *schizophrenia*. But *I* heard the voice too, and I sure as heck never heard of shared schizophrenia.

Chloe empties the last of the wine into our glasses. 'I was terrified I was losing my marbles, so – without telling Stuart – I visited three separate doctors, had a brain scan, the works. Nothing sinister showed up. I was Stuart's round-the-clock carer, he was going downhill fast, so two of the three consultants put it down to stress. One told me the voices were caused by an unfulfilled yearning for children. I didn't go back to him.'

I drink the wine. I puff on the cigarette. 'So apart from me, nobody else has heard them?'

'That's right. I – I can't tell you how relieved I was, last Saturday, when I saw you'd heard them too. How less lonely I felt. *God*, just to be able to discuss them like this, without being afraid you'll think I'm a nut . . . You've got no idea, Gordon.'

Blue eyes. Grey eyes. 'Hence my invitation?'

A shy little smile. 'Not the only reason. Don't feel exploited.'

'I don't. Hey, Bergerac sensed them, too. He legged it.' I pour myself coffee from the silver pot. 'Why do you stay here, Chloe? Why don't you sell up and move somewhere . . . less haunted?'

Chloe grimaces the way I've noticed she does when faced with a thorny question. 'Slade House is home. I feel safe here, and . . . it's not as if Norah and Jonah go "*Wooooooh*" or drip ectoplasm or write scary messages in mirrors. I . . . I'm not even sure they know I'm here. Yes, I hear them, once or twice, every one or two days, but they're just going about their business.' Chloe balances a teaspoon on a dish. 'There's one other voice I call Eeyore because he's always so negative, but I've only heard him a handful of times. He mumbles things like "*They're liars*" or "*Run away*" or stuff that makes no sense, and I suppose he's a bit disconcerting, but he wouldn't qualify as a poltergeist. I'm not leaving Slade House just because of him.'

Bergerac rubs his back against my shins. I hadn't noticed him come back in. 'I still think you're made of sterner stuff than most people, Chloe. I mean . . . well . . . *ghosts.*'

Chloe sighs. 'Some people keep boa constrictors, or tarantulas; surely that's weirder and scarier and riskier than my innocuous housemates? I'm not even convinced they're real "ghosts" at all.'

'Innocuous' means 'harmless', if I'm not wrong. 'If they're not ghosts, what are they?'

'My theory is that they're ordinary children, living in their own time, doing their thing, whom I overhear. Like the telephone lines of our times have crossed. The wall between our "now" and their "now" is thin. That's all.'

The big window shows a reflected kitchen with a ghostly Chloe and me superimposed onto a dark garden. 'If I hadn't heard them myself,' I say, 'I'd be thinking you'd watched too many episodes of *Tales of the Unexpected* or something. But . . . I *did* hear them. Have you thought of finding out who used to live in Slade House? Maybe you'd find a pair of twins called Jonah and Norah.'

She rolls up her napkin. 'I've thought about it, but since Stuart died, I just haven't had the get-up-and-go.' Chloe makes an apologetic face. I realise I want to kiss it.

Bergerac nestles into my crotch. May his claws stay retracted. 'The property records at the town archives go back to the 1860s,' I tell Chloe. 'We – CID, I mean – consult them now and then. I've got a tame archivist called Leon who looks into certain matters for me, without asking the whys and wherefores. A big old house like this leaves footprints in local history. Shall I have a quiet word?'

'First a door fixer, now an archivist.' Chloe looks impressed. 'You're a one-man *Yellow Pages*. Yes please. I'd be jolly grateful.'

'Leave it with me.' I stroke Bergerac. He purrs.

My host reties her hair. 'Honestly, Gordon. Most men would be dashing for the door by now.'

I breathe out a cloud of smoke. 'I'm not most men.'

Me and Chloe look at each other longer than you're normally allowed to. She reaches over and puts my dessert plate onto hers. 'I *knew* that telephoning you earlier was a smart move.'

I wish I had a snappier line than 'More coffee?'

'Golly, no. I shan't be able to sleep for *hours*.'

Exactly, I think. 'Then let me do the washing-up.'

'That's why God made dishwashers, my friend.'

I notice her wedding ring is off. 'Then I'm jobless.'

Blue eyes. Grey eyes. 'Not necessarily.'

Rasping and gasping for breath, soaked, salty and sticky, I collapse onto her pillow. I'm fed, I'm fed, I'm fed, and the finest thing to be in God's glorious creation is a youngish well-fed male. We just lie there for a while until our breathing and heart rates slow down a little. I say, 'If you let me have a rerun, I'll pace myself a bit better.' Chloe tells me, 'Make an appointment, I'll see if I can *squeeze* you in,' which makes me laugh so my deflating truncheon slips out. She gives me a fistful of tissues and rolls onto her side, dabbing her own loins and wrapping herself in the gluey sheet. She didn't tell me to use a condom, so I didn't: a bit of a risk, but it's her risk, not mine, and any successful businessman'll tell you, risk transfer is the name of the game. The four-poster bed is hung with maroon curtains so everything's warm and dark and smothered. I tell her, 'Well. Your triple mortice lock most definitely meets industry standards.'

She biffs me gently with the back of her hand.

'Serious crime, that – assaulting a police officer.'

'Ooh. Will you get out your handcuffs?'

'Only in my smuttiest dreams.'

Chloe kisses my nipple. 'Then sleep.'

'Fat chance of that, lying next to a naked goddess.'

She kisses my eyelids. 'Sweet dreams, Detective.'

I yawn, enormously. 'I'm honestly not sleepy . . .'

Next time I wake, she's gone. My meat and two veg are simmering nicely. In the walls, ancient plumbing's groaning, and water's slapping the floor of a nearby shower. I find my watch under a pillow: 1.30. The wee small hours. No problem, it's Sunday. I'm not due in to the office till Tuesday. Bugger Tuesday. Bugger work. Bugger the Malik Enquiry. Bugger Trevor Doolan. Bugger the Great British Public. Me and Chloe should stay in and do this all Sunday, all week, all month . . . Only something's niggling me. What? A thought. This one: why is this classy, clever, sexy-as-hell female falling into bed with a guy she hardly knows? This happens in Pornland or in men's bullshittery, but here in the real world, women like Chloe simply don't shag men on a second encounter. Do they?

Hang on, Gordon Edmonds, hang on. 'Second encounter'? This is your *fifth* visit to Slade House, you plonker. Count the meals: on the first Saturday, Chloe cooked steak; second Saturday, cod on shredded potatoes; venison and Guinness pie on the third; last week was pheasant; and tonight, roast beef. There. See? Five dinners, five Saturdays, five bottles of wine, and five long talks for hours about big stuff and small stuff and stuff in between: childhoods, attitudes, politics; her deceased husband and my ex-wife; John Ruskin, the Victorian scholar of art. You've been phoning each other every night just to say 'Goodnight' and 'Sweet dreams' and 'Can't wait till Saturday'. It's not been a long courtship, true, but it's been intense, sincere and not remotely slutty or porny. You're a good-looking cop and you're obviously amazing in bed. What's the problem? Chloe Albertina Chetwynd loves you.

I don't love her, not yet, but love grows out of sex, in my experience. The more you get into a woman, the more you get into her. Who knows? We could end up getting married. Imagine owning Slade House, or half owning it. Who cares about three little spooks? The fact that I hear them makes me special in Chloe's eyes. Slade House is *way* bigger than Trevor Doolan's executive home up on his hill with his well-paid Conservative Club neighbours. If the Malik Enquiry throws me to the wolves, Slade House'd be my lifeboat, my fuck-off money. How much is it worth? £100,000? £120,000? Fortunes change hands every day, all the time, via business, via the football pools, via crime or, yes, via marriage. I'll give Chloe security and fill the man-shaped hole in her life; she'll offer me financial security.

Seems like a fair deal. '*Goooooorrrrrr*-donnn!' Her voice finds me from a nearby room. 'Are you awake?'

I shout back to her, 'I am now – where are you?'

'*Dans la douche*, and I can't un*screw* this shampoo . . .'

You cheeky little minx. 'Oh, can't you indeed?'

'I'm a damsel in distress, Gordon. Up the stairs.'

There's a man's furry brown dressing gown on the bed. Probably Stuart's, but hey, now I've had his widow, why should he care if I have his dressing gown as well? I put it on, slide off the bed and slip through the thick red drapes, cross the odd round room and find myself on a square landing. To my left's a grandfather clock, to my right, stairs lead down to the hallway, and up ahead, more stairs climb past some pictures to a pale door at the top of the house where a soapy Chloe Chetwynd awaits her Knight in Shining Armour. 'Are you coming, Gordon?' Oh, I will be, I will be. Up I climb, two steps at a time, past a portrait of a teenager in a beaten-up leather jacket, with dark oily hair and narrow eyes like he's half Chinese. The next picture is of a young woman dolled up to the nines and with a honey-blonde hairdo like a backing singer from a sixties girl band. She's got a dreamy smile that reminds me of Julie when she wasn't being a neurotic bitch so I stop and brush her lips with mine, just 'cause I can. The third portrait up from the landing's of a boy of about thirteen. Sandy hair, big nose, sulky, not at ease in his skin, or that tweed jacket and bow tie that you suspect his pushy mother made him—

It's Nathan Bishop. It can't be. It is. My heart's juddering and I feel sick and weightless. Nathan Bishop, as seen by Fred Pink in Slade Alley in 1979. Nathan Bishop, whose photo Fred Pink cut out of the newspaper. Trevor Doolan got Debs to photocopy it and pin it above our desks, so Famous Fred Pink could see how seriously the Thames Valley Force was taking his lead. *She's lying*, says a sulky voice in my ear canal, clear as anything. I jump; nearly fall; crouch; look round. Nobody. *She'll take your life, and more . . .*

Stairs going up; stairs going down; nobody's here.

I try to un-tense myself. I imagined it. That's all.

You may find a weapon in the cracks, says the voice.

This one's not like Jonah or Norah in the kitchen. This voice is addressing me. I don't know how I know but I know.

The cracks they throw the scraps down, says the boy.

Cracks? Scraps? Weapon? I manage to mutter, 'Who are you?' but as I'm saying it to the portrait of Nathan Bishop, the smarter part of me thinks it knows.

I'm not a lot, says the boy. *I'm my own leftovers.*

'Why will I' – what am I doing, talking to a picture of a vanished boy? – 'why'll I need a weapon?'

The grandfather clock's tocking, far far below.

It's all in my head. It's not. Each word's a throb of pain.

For you, it's too late, says the boy. *But pass it on.*

'Pass it on to who?' I ask the voice that may or may not be real.

The next guest . . . I'm finished now . . . I'm all used up.

I say, 'Hello?' but the boy's gone. I crawl backwards up the stairs, away from Nathan Bishop's portrait, until my eyes lock onto the next one which I also recognise instantly 'cause it's me, Gordon Edmonds. I ought to be totally freaked out by this, but there's only so many shocks you can take before your, I dunno, circuits burn out. So I just gape, like a total bloody lemon. I gape at the more-real-than-real picture of gaping Gordon Edmonds, in a brown furry dressing gown, with my buzz-cut hair, my retreating hairline, my kind-of-leaner-fitter-better-looking-Phil-Collins face, with bloody creepy skin-tone blanks where my eyes should be. I stare until I think, *You should get out of this house. You don't know what you're dealing with.* But that's idiotic as well as chickenshit. Run off, 'cause Chloe painted your portrait? I try to think, but it's not easy. My brain's sort of numb. If Chloe painted my portrait, she painted the others. If Chloe painted the others, she painted Nathan Bishop. Meaning she lied about not knowing his name. Meaning . . .

Chloe's a killer? Get a grip. I've interviewed three or four serial killers, and Chloe's nothing like those faeces-gobbling fucks. Look again. Yes, Chloe painted me as a surprise, but it doesn't follow that she painted the other pictures. The other pictures look like they were painted a long time ago. They must have been hanging here when Chloe and Stuart bought the place from the Pitts. That explains it. Sort of. They don't have titles or signatures, so Chloe couldn't've known she's passed Nathan Bishop every time she uses these stairs. And I didn't show her the boy's picture last week in the garden; all I did was tell her his name.

What about the voice I just heard, warning me to get out?

What about it? Just 'cause you hear a ghostly voice, that doesn't mean you have to take what it says as Gospel. Maybe the voice I just heard wasn't Nathan Bishop but the one Chloe called Eeyore. Anyway, how do I *know* I heard it? What if I only imagined it?

Here's what you do: get Chloe out of the shower, tell her she owns a portrait of Nathan Bishop, assure her she's not a suspect, and first thing tomorrow call Chief Super Doolan at home. He won't be best pleased at first, and it'll be a bit embarrassing when everyone at the station discovers I've been shagging Chloe, but once Doolan learns that Fred Pink's lead might not be such a neon-bright red herring after all, he'll change his tune soon enough.

Sorted, then. In we go.

But on the other side of the pale door, I find not a bathroom with Chloe in a shower, but a long dark attic. A long dark attic that's some sort of . . . *prison*? That's sure as hell what it looks like. Three-quarters of it's caged off by thick, sturdy bars, an inch thick and an inch apart. I can't see how far back the attic goes 'cause it's so dark. A faint bit of light comes in from two skylights, on the 'free' side of the bars above where I am, but that's it. The attic smells of bad breath and pine disinfectant, a lot like the cells down the station. My thumb finds a switch to flick, and a light comes on behind the bars. It's a weak bulb, high up. I make out a bed, a washbasin, a sofa, a table, a chair, a toilet cubicle with the door ajar, an exercise bike and someone stirring on the bed, half hidden in blankets and shadow. The attic's only about five metres wide but it goes back a long way, maybe the full width of Slade House. I press my face against the bars to peer in the best I can and I say, 'Hello?'

He or she – I can't see which – doesn't reply. A mad relative? How legal is any of this? I'm going to have to report it in the morning.

I try again. 'Hello? What're you doing up here?'

I hear breathing, and the camp-bed squeaks.

'Do you speak English? Do you need any help? Do—'

A woman's voice cuts in: 'Are you real?' A brittle voice.

Not the sanest opening question. The bed's halfway down the attic, and I can't see much – a cheekbone, a hand, a shoulder, a flop of grey hair. 'My name's Gordon Edmonds, and yes, I'm real.'

She sits up in bed and hugs her knees. 'Dream-people always say they're real, so pardon me for not believing you.' The woman sounds frail and sad but well spoken. 'Once I dreamed that Charlie Chaplin came to rescue me with a pair of giant nail clippers.' She squints my way with a face that hasn't smiled for years. 'Vyvyan Ayrs drilled a hole in the roof, once. I climbed out of the hole and he strapped me onto his hang-glider, and we flew over the English Channel to Zedelghem. I cried when I woke up.' A radiator groans. 'Gordon Edmonds. You're new.'

'Yes, I am.' She's talking like a mental case. 'So . . . are you a patient?'

She scowls. 'If you're real, you'll know who I am.'

'Not true, I'm afraid. I'm real, and I don't know you.'

The woman's voice turns harsher: 'The Monster wants me to think I'm being rescued, doesn't she? It's her little entertainment. Tell her I'm not playing.'

'*Who* wants you to think you're being rescued?'

'The Monster's the Monster. I don't say her name.'

Her name? A nasty thought creeps up − Chloe − but there'll be a logical explanation. 'Sweetheart, I'm a copper. Detective Inspector Gordon Edmonds, Thames Valley Force, CID. Can you just tell me why you're here? Or at least, why you think you're here?'

'A detective in a dressing gown. Undercover, is it?'

'It doesn't bloody matter what I've got on − I'm a copper.'

She gets out of bed and floats towards the bars in a nightie. 'Liar.'

I step back, just in case she's got a knife. 'Love, *please*. I . . . just want to know what the story is. Tell me your name at least.'

One mad eye appears in the inch between two bars. 'Rita.'

The sentence says itself like a conjurer's hanky pulled out of my mouth: 'Oh, sweet bloody hell, don't tell me you're Rita Bishop . . .'

The woman blinks. 'Yes. As you know perfectly well.'

I peer closer, and summon up the other photocopied picture Debs pinned above our desks. Oh, Jesus. Rita

Bishop's aged, badly, but it's her. 'After all these years' – her breath smells vinegary – 'does the Monster downstairs still get a kick from these pantomimes?'

I feel like I've lost half my blood. 'Have you' – I'm afraid of the answer – 'have you been in this attic since 1979?'

'No,' she sneers. 'First they hid me away in Buckingham Palace; then a fortune-teller's booth on Brighton pier; then Willy Wonka's—'

'O*kay*! Okay.' I'm trembling. 'Where's Nathan? Your son?'

Rita Bishop shuts her eyes and forces out her words: 'Ask *her*! Ask Lady Norah Grayer, or whatever name she's going by this week. She's the one who lured us to Slade House; who drugged us; who locked us up; who took Nathan away; who won't even tell me if my son's still alive or not!' She folds over and lies in a silent crying heap.

My mind's jolted and clattery: Chloe Chetywnd? Norah Grayer? Same woman? How? *How?* The paintings? Why? Why bring a CID officer up to bed? Why lure him up the stairs where he'll see the paintings? Makes no sense. What I *do* know is that Slade House isn't a police station, a prison or a psychiatric ward, and it looks like we have a case of illegal imprisonment here. Ordinarily – ha, 'ordinarily' – I'd go back to my car, radio for backup and warrants and return in a couple of hours, but in this mad bugger's scenario, where I may – *may* – have just shagged a thirty-one-year-old killer-slash-abductress-slash-whatever-the-fuck-she-is, I'd rather get Rita Bishop safely away first and call in a Code 10 to Slade House after. If I'm wrong and

Trevor Doolan de-bollocks me then so be it. 'Mrs Bishop. Do you know where the key is?'

She's still a softly sobbing mess on the floor.

I notice the sound of the shower's stopped.

'Mrs Bishop – help me help you – *please.*'

The woman lifts her head and fires hate-rays at me: 'As if you'll just unlock this door after nine years. As *if.*'

For Chrissakes. 'If I am who I say I am, you'll be out of Slade House in two minutes and I swear on all that's holy, Mrs Bishop, I'll have armed officers in here within thirty minutes and "the Monster" in custody, and in the morning CID and Scotland Yard *and* Forensics on Nathan's trail, so will you *please* just *tell me* where the key is? Right now I'm your only chance of seeing your son again.'

Something in my voice persuades Rita Bishop to give me a chance. She sits up. 'The key's on the hook. Right behind you. It amuses the Monster that I can see it.'

I turn round: a long, thin, shiny key. I take it, and fumble, and drop the thing. It hits the floorboard with a pure note. I pick it up and find the steel plate in the cage door and push the key into the keyhole. It's well oiled and the door swings open and Rita Bishop staggers to her feet and backs off and sways forwards and stares like she can't believe it. 'Come on, Mrs Bishop,' I whisper, 'out you come. We're leaving.'

The prisoner takes uncertain steps to the cage door where she grips my hand, and steps out. 'I, I . . .' Her breathing's all raspy.

'Easy does it,' I tell her. 'It's okay. Do you know if . . . if "she", "they", if they've got weapons?'

Rita Bishop can't answer. She's gripping my dressing gown, quivering. 'Promise me, *promise me*, I'm not dreaming you.'

'I promise. Let's go.'

Her fingers dig into my wrist. 'And you're not dreaming me?'

I stay patient; if I'd been locked up for nine years, I'd be off my rocker too. 'I guarantee it. Now let's get out of here.'

She releases me. 'Look at this, Detective.'

'Mrs Bishop, we need to leave.'

Ignoring me, she holds up a lighter.

Her thumb flicks and a thin flame . . .

. . . grows longer, paler and still as a freeze-frame. It's not a lighter any more, it's a candle, on a chunky metal base with writing all over it, Arabic or Hebrew or Foreign. The cage has gone. All the furniture's gone. Rita Bishop's gone. The candle's the only source of light. The shrunken attic's black as inside a coffin deep inside a blocked-up cave. I'm kneeling, I'm paralysed, and I don't know what's happening. I try to move but no joy. Not even a finger. Not even my tongue. My body's the cage now, and I'm the one locked in. The only things working are my eyes and my brain. Work it out, then. Nerve gas? A stroke? I've been Mickey Finned? God only knows. Clues, then, Detective? There're three faces in the dark. Straight ahead, across the candle, there's me in a dead man's dressing gown. A mirror, obviously. On my left there's Chloe, in a hooded padded robe thing. On my right there's . . . a male Chloe. Chloe's twin, I'm guessing – this blond guy, dressed in a robe thing like Chloe's, handsome in a sort of gay model Hitler Youth way. Neither of them is moving. A few inches from the candle flame there's a brownish moth, just frozen in the air, frozen in time. I'm not dreaming. That's about all I'm sure of. So is this the story of how Gordon Edmonds lost his mind?

Time passes. I don't know how much. The candle hisses and its white flame sways this way and that. The moth flaps around, in and out of the dark; now I see it, now I don't. 'You're smirking, Brother,' says Chloe, if that's her real name. This woman has the same face as the one who served me tiramisu but while her voice before was smooth and woollen, now it's a rusty jackknife.

'I am not smirking,' objects the man, moving his legs like they've got pins and needles.

I try to move too. I still can't. I try to speak. I can't.

'You're a damned liar, Jonah,' says Chloe. She holds up her hands like they're a pair of gloves she can't make up her mind about. '*I* didn't smirk when you serviced that hair-dresser two cycles ago. And you really *did* exchange fluids; I only threw this dog-in-heat –' she gives me a disgusted, sideways look '– an imaginary bone.'

'*If* I smiled,' says the man, 'it was a smile of pride at your performance in my sub-orison. You played the neurotic widow to perfection. The attic cage was one of my finest *mises-en-scène*, I think we'll agree, but Meryl Streep herself could not have delivered the role of poor Mrs Bishop with finer aplomb. Why, *I* scarcely noticed the prickly creature, all those years ago. Her voice hurt my ears. Why the long face, Sister? Yet another Open Day has gone swimmingly, our operandi has proven itself robust, our pheasant is plucked and basted, yet you're looking all . . . vinegary.'

'The operandi is an improvised hotchpotch, too reliant—'

'Norah, I beg you, we're about to dine; can't we just—'

'—*too* reliant upon luck, Jonah. Upon nothing going wrong.'

The man – Jonah – looks at his sister – Norah – with fond smugness. 'For fifty-four years, our souls have wandered that big wide world out there, possessing whatever bodies we want, living whatever lives we wish, while our fellow birth-Victorians are all dead or dying out. We live on. The operandi *works*.'

'The operandi works pro*v*ided our birth-bodies remain here in the lacuna, freeze-dried against world-time, anchoring our souls in life. The operandi works pro*v*ided we recharge the lacuna every nine years by luring a gullible Engifted into a suitable orison. The operandi works pro*v*ided our guests can be duped, banjaxed and drawn into the lacuna. Too many *provided*s, Jonah. Yes, our luck's held so far. It can't hold forever, and it won't.'

I've got no idea what they're on about, but Jonah looks

properly pissed off. 'Why this illuminating lecture now, Sister?'

'We need to make the operandi proof against mischance and enemies.'

'What enemies? Thanks to my insistence on isolation, not even the Shaded Way know about us. Our life-support system works: why tamper with it? Now, supper is served.' Jonah looks my way. 'That would be you, Detective Plod.'

I try but I can't move, or fight, or beg. I can't even shit myself.

'You've stopped breathing,' Jonah tells me, matter-of-factly.

No no no, I must be breathing, I think. *I'm still conscious.*

'Not for much longer,' replies Jonah. 'After four minutes without oxygen, brain damage becomes irreversible, and although I don't have my watch on me, I'd say you've had two. You'd die after six minutes, but we intervene prior to the final agony. We're not sadists.'

I feel like I'm plunging upwards. *What did I do to deserve this?*

'What does "deserve" have to do with anything?' Norah Grayer lifts her sharp eyebrows. 'Did the pig whose smoked flesh you ate at breakfast "deserve" her fate? The question's irrelevant. You desired bacon and she couldn't escape the abbatoir. We desire your soul to power our operandi, and you can't escape our lacuna. That's it.'

Men who scare easily don't last long in the force, but

now I'm scared as hell. Although religion always struck me as daft, suddenly it's all I've got: *If they're soul-stealers, pray to God.* How does it go? *Our Father . . .*

'Splendid idea,' says Jonah. 'I'll do you a deal, Detective Inspector. If you recite the Lord's Prayer from start to finish − Book of Common Prayer version − you win a Get Out of Jail Free card. Go on. See how far you get.'

'This is juvenile, Brother,' sighs Norah.

'Fair's fair, he should have a chance. On your marks, Plod; get set; "*Our Father, which art in heaven*" . . . Go on.'

This Jonah's a skunk and a snake, but I've got no choice. '*Our Father, which art in heaven, hallowed be thou name—*'

'Was that a "*thou*" or a "*thy*" you quoth?' asks Jonah. I have to play this bastard's game. I think, '*Thy.*'

'Bravo! Onwards, onwards. "*Hallowed be* thy *name*".'

What's next? '*Thy kingdom come, thy will be done on earth, as it is in heaven. Give us this day our daily bread, and lead us not into temptation, and forgive us our trespassers, as we—*'

'Ooooo! "Trespass*ers*" as in "Git orf my larrrnd!" or "trespass*es*" as in "transgressions"? Former or latter? Person or act?'

Jesus, I want to glass his sodding face. I think, '*The act.*'

'Plod's on a roll! *Forgive us our trespasses . . .*'

'*As we forgive those who . . . who . . . who . . .*'

'What's this? A thought-stutter or an owl impression?'

'*Who trespass against us. For thine is the kingdom, the power and the glory, forever and ever, Amen.*' I've done it. I look at him.

The bastard actually smiles. 'Alas, it's "*forgive* 'them that' *trespass against us*"; temptation comes after trespasses; and you forgot the "*deliver us from evil*" bit. Ironically.'

I'm going to die.

This hour.

Now. Me.

'The point of that little interlude being . . . ?' asks Norah.

'A sprinkle of last-minute despair gives a soul an agreeably earthy aftertaste. Ready when you are, Sister?'

Norah mutters, 'I'm always ready,' and the Grayer twins begin tracing symbols in the air. They're chanting, too, a chant in a language I don't know, and something appears above the candle flame, a bit above eye level: a bruise in the air, a glowing lump, lit reddish from inside, beating like a heart, big as a brain. Worms or roots or veins snake out from it. Some grow towards the twins, and several come my way and I try to pull my head back or swat them away or even shriek or shut my eyes but I can't; they enter my mouth, my ears, my nostrils, like sharp tiny fingers, and get to work inside me. I feel a nail of pain sink into my forehead, and in the mirror I see a black dot there . . . Not blood. Seconds pass. Something oozes out and hovers there, a blob the size and shape of a golf ball, right in front of my eyes. It's almost see-through, like gel, or egg white, and filled with shiny grains of dust, or galaxies, or . . .

God, it's beautiful.

Jesus, it shimmers.

It's alive, it's mine . . .

. . . the twins' faces loom up, Jonah to my left, Norah to my right, smooth-skinned, hungry, pursing their lips like whistlers, sucking, so sharply, that my soul – what else could it be? – is slowly but surely stretched like Blu-Tack. Half my soul streams like smoke into Norah's mouth and half into Jonah's. I'd sob, if I could, or I'd say *I'll get you I'll kill you I'll make you pay*, but I'm just the residue of Gordon Edmonds now. I'm his husk. I'm his flesh-and-skin suit. The twins gasp and let out soft groans like junkies shooting up when the drug hits the bloodstream. Now there's a rushing noise louder than the end of the world. Now it's quiet like the morning after the end of the world. The floating brain-thing's gone; its air-veins are gone too. Like nothing was ever there. The Grayer twins kneel across the candle from each other, as still as the flame that never moves. The mirror's empty. Look at the scorched tiny papery scrap. There, on the floorboard. That was a moth, once.

OINK

OINK

1997

'Five,' pronounces Axel Hardwick, astrophysics postgrad, corduroy-clad, hair short, black and curly, real name Alan not Axel, but he thinks Axel makes him sound more Guns N' Roses. Axel looks at us as if *we*'re the ones who haven't bothered turning up. 'Some shrinkage is inevitable as the dead wood drops out, but a head count of five, at this point in the term, is frankly dismal.' There's a beery racket booming up the stairs from the main bar below and my mind sort of floats off, and I wonder if I'd have met more people if I'd joined the Photography Society in Freshers' Week instead of the Paranormal Society, like I meant to. But then I wouldn't have met Todd.

Todd Cosgrove, second year maths, a shyish elfish guy, black coat, white T-shirt, maroon jeans, Camel boots, vice president of ParaSoc, fan of the Smiths. Across the table from me, Todd sips his Newcastle Brown Ale. His mad, quiffy hair's brown, too, brown like strong stewed tea before you add the milk. Todd lives with his parents here in town but he's not creepy or helpless, he's bright and kind and strong, so there's probably a good reason why he still lives at home. My mouth and brain seize up if I try to speak with him, but when I shut my eyes at night, Todd's there. It's crazy. But like every love song in the history of love songs says, love is crazy.

'The walk may have deterred some of the waverers,' opines Angelica Gibbons. Definitely more Gibbons than Angelica, she's a second year studying anthropology, has floppy indigo hair, Doc Martens, dresses like a fortune-teller, and is as big-boned as me. I thought we might be friends, but when we only scored 18 per cent on the telepathy test she blamed me and said I had 'no psychic potential whatsoever'. It was the way she said 'whatsoever'.

Axel scowls. 'The Fox and Hounds is a twenty-minute walk from campus. Tops. I refuse to eat into ParaSoc's budget by laying on fleets of buses for a two-mile walk.' He starts spinning a beer mat. A leprechaun on an enamelled Guinness ad over the fireplace catches my eye. He's playing his fiddle for a dancing toucan.

'I completely agree, Axel,' says Angelica. 'I'm just saying.'

'Maybe a gang of them are coming but got lost *en masse*, like.' Lance Arnott, final year philosophy, dandruff, Pink Floyd *The Wall* T-shirt, pongs of hamburgers. Lance made a pass at me at the Roman ruins at Silchester. Frightmare on Elm Street or what? I lied about a boyfriend in Malvern, but he thinks I'm just playing hard to get. He turns to Fern: 'Where's that mate of yours this week, Ferny?'

Fern Penhaligon, first year like me but doing drama, Rapunzel hair, slim as a model, Cornish-born, Chelsea-bred, Alexander McQueen jeans, Union Jack parka and here to 'research the supernatural' for a stage version of *Ghost* that she's starring in, curls her lip. 'It's Fern; and which "mate" do you mean?' She sips the Cointreau she let Lance buy her, but he's a bigger dick than he acts if he thinks he's in with a chance.

'The one who came to Saint Aelfric's. The one with the huge gazonking' – Lance mimes a pair of breasts – 'personality. The *Waylsh* one.'

Fern swirls ice cubes round her glass. 'Yasmin, you mean.'

'*Yasmin*. Get a better offer tonight, did she? Eh? *Boyo?*' Lance gurns at Todd. I send Todd a telepathic message saying, *Ignore Lance, he's a plonker*. And lo and behold, Todd ignores Lance, so maybe it's actually Angelica who has no psychic potential 'whatsoever'. I try again: *Look at my fingernails, Todd, I painted them peacock blue*. But Todd's got his apple-pip brown eyes on Fern, who's explaining that her absent friend Yasmin was underwhelmed by the last field trip.

'"Underwhelmed"?' Axel stops spinning his beer mat. 'By any standard metric, Saint Aelfric's is England's most haunted church.'

Fern shrugs. 'She was hoping to catch a glimpse of an actual ghost instead of catching a head cold.'

'Paranormal entities don't come when you whistle,' Angelica tells her. 'They're not like live-in Filipino maids.'

I'd be stung by that, but for Fern it's water off a duck's back. 'It's "Filipin*a*", for females, you'll find – and I'd know, of course, being so *awfully, frightfully* posh.' Fern places one of her Gauloises cigarettes between her lips and lights it.

Angelica's squished like a bug and I think, *Direct hit!* and Fern gives me a knowing look.

'Well, I'm not hanging about any longer for people who aren't coming or who don't show up on time,' announces Axel, passing around a thin wodge of printouts headed *Paranormal Society Field Trip Briefing, 25 October 1997* and subtitled *The Slade Alley Vanishings.* Underneath are two photographs. The top picture's actually split into two: the left half is a grainy school photo of a boy, about twelve, with geeky hair and a nose on the wrong side of large; the right half shows a strict-looking woman in her late thirties, dark hair bunched up, thin, wearing a blouse with a frilly neck, pearls and a cardigan. Mother and son, you can tell at a glance. Neither was comfortable looking into a camera. The caption reads, *Nathan and Rita Bishop: last seen in Slade Alley, Saturday, 27 October, 1979.* The bottom picture shows a man of thirty or so, grinning at the camera, sinking a beer and dressed like a cop from *Miami Vice*, though he's going bald and he isn't thin. His caption reads, *Detective Inspector Gordon Edmonds: last seen entering Slade Alley, Saturday, 29 October, 1988.* So I was right: he is a cop. At the foot of the page is *Copyright Axel Hardwick 1997.* That's it.

'"The Slade Alley Vanishings",' reads Lance. 'Cool.'

'Uh, I *think* we can all read the title,' says Angelica.

'The case study would have taken an age to write down in all its detail,' says Axel, 'so I'm going to brief you all verbally.'

'It was a dark and stormy night,' says Lance in a comedy Somerset accent.

'If you're not serious about this,' Angelica tells him, 'you—'

'Just cranking up the atmosphere a bit. Go on, Axel.'

Axel stares at Lance to tell him, *Grow up.* 'It begins eighteen years ago, in early November 1979. A pissed-off landlord was banging on the door of a property he was renting to Rita Bishop, divorced mother of Nathan, pictured here. The rent cheque had bounced. Again. A neighbour told the landlord that he hadn't seen either Rita Bishop or her son for at least ten days. Hearing this, the landlord notified the police, who found out that Nathan hadn't been at school since the last Friday in October. A half-arsed search ensued. Why half-arsed? Because Rita Bishop had dual British–Canadian citizenship, an ex-husband living in Zimbabwe-slash-Rhodesia, and mounting debts. The police assumed she'd done a runner for financial reasons and filed the case in the WGT file.'

Fern flicks her mane of hair. '"WGT"?'

'It stands for "Who Gives a Toss?".' Axel sips his bitter while Angelica acts all amused. 'Next, fast-forward to September 1988. A patient named Fred Pink wakes up from a coma in the unit at the Royal Berkshire Hospital, nine years after being knocked into oblivion by a drunk taxi driver on Westwood Road.'

'Westwood Road's this road, right?' I ask.

'It was on tonight's rendezvous sheet,' says Angelica.

Stupid moo. I sip my Diet Coke, wishing I were Fern so I could administer a barbed put-down. And pull guys. Like Todd. Just for example.

'Fred Pink began working through all the back copies of the local newspaper, to see what he'd missed during what he calls his Big Sleep. Pretty soon, he found a picture of the missing Rita and Nathan Bishop. They looked familiar. Why? Because back in 1979, just before the minicab driver hit him, Fred Pink had spoken with Rita Bishop at the Cranbury Avenue entrance to Slade Alley, one street up from Westwood Road. She'd asked if he knew where Lady Norah Grayer lived. Fred Pink said no, walked down the alley, and at the far end got knocked down by the taxi.'

'Bang! Crash! Wallop!' Lance rearranges his genitals without a flicker of embarrassment.

'No disrespect to Mr Pink,' says Todd, 'but how trustworthy a witness was he?' His voice has a soft yokel twang but it's actually quite sexy.

Axel's nod means *Good question.* 'The police were sceptical too. This neighbourhood isn't rough, but it certainly isn't rich. If a genuine "lady" had her "residence" here, she'd stick out like a very posh sore thumb. Even so, CID didn't want Fred Pink to feel brushed off, so they sent a man to give Slade Alley the once-over. Enter Detective Inspector Gordon Edmonds.' Axel taps the second photograph on the A4 sheet. 'On October twenty-second, 1988, he entered Slade Alley and found a door in the wall. It was open. He went in, and found a garden and a "substantial property" called Slade House.'

'And living in Slade House was Lady Grayer?' asks Angelica, looping her finger through her indigo hair.

'No. By 1988, the owner was a young widow called Chloe Chetwynd. Edmonds's brief report – my primary source for tonight's field trip – makes it clear that Chloe Chetwynd knew nothing about a Lady Grayer or the missing Bishops.'

'Ah, but she would say that, wouldn't she?' Fern stubs out her cigarette. 'In racy Victorian novels, beware of young widows. Especially attractive ones.'

'Pity no one told Gordon Edmonds that,' says Axel. 'The following Saturday he went back to Slade House. Apparently he'd recommended a security contractor to Chloe Chetwynd to fix that garden door, and she asked him to check the workmanship. A witness saw him park his car on Westwood Road at 6 p.m. –' Axel can't resist a dramatic pause '– but Detective Inspector Edmonds was never seen again.'

'When a cop goes missing,' says Angelica, 'the fuzz don't rest until they've found their man. The media join in, too.'

'True,' replies Axel. 'And Gordon Edmonds did make the front pages, for a few days. Theories about an IRA kidnapping or a suicide pact kept the story on the boil for a while, but when Edmonds refused to show up either dead or alive, pictures of Lady Di's arse or the Poll Tax riots or the Divorce of the Day reclaimed their rightful place on the front page of the *News of the Screws,* and Detective Inspector Edmonds fell off the radar.'

Angelica asks, 'What was Chloe Chetwynd's version of events?'

'In a curious twist to the tale,' says Axel, 'Chloe Chetwynd was never tracked down by the investigators.'

We look at each other, wondering what we've missed.

'Hang on a mo,' says Lance. 'So who answered the door at Slade House when the cops went looking for Gordon Edmonds?'

'In yet another curious twist' – Axel sips his beer – 'Slade House turned out to be just as elusive as Chloe Chetwynd.'

'Whoa, whoa, whoa,' says Lance. 'The *house* disappeared?'

'Big stone houses,' Fern points out, 'don't *nor*mally melt into the fog.'

Axel sniffs. 'Last time I looked, we're the *Para*normal Society.'

Down in the bar a fruit machine vomits out a slug of coins.

'Proper X-File, this is,' says Lance, teetering on his chair.

'What if,' proposes Fern, 'Gordon Edmonds made Slade House up in his notes – and invented Chloe Chetwynd, too?'

'Why risk so much on such a flimsy lie?' asks Angelica.

'No idea,' states Fern. 'Nervous breakdown? Serial fanta-sist? Who knows? But which is likelier, people, really: fabricated police records or a house going *pooff*, in viola-tion of the laws of physics?'

'What did that security contractor guy say?' asks Todd.

Axel's pretending not to enjoy this but he is. 'He swore blind that nobody ever contacted him about a Slade House: neither a Chloe Chetwynd nor a Detective Inspector Edmonds.'

'Murderers have been known to lie,' says Angelica.

'CID investigated him,' says Axel, 'and every locksmith, builder, whatever, in the area too – and found zilch, nada, niente, sod all. Nobody had worked at any Slade House in, or near, Westwood Road.'

Todd asks, 'Was the Slade Alley connection between Gordon Edmonds's disappearance in 1988 and the Bishops' disappearance in 1979 made public at the time?'

Axel shakes his head. 'The factoid was suppressed. The cops didn't want Slade Alley to become a magnet for true-crime nuts.'

'Typical of the fascist pigs to repress the truth,' says Angelica.

I'd like to ask Angelica how safe she thinks she'd be in a society without any police at all, but I don't have the nerve. Todd asks, 'How did *you* link the two disappearances, Axel?'

'An informant brought it to my attention,' Axel looks a bit cagey, 'and suggested that ParaSoc take a closer look.'

'What informant?' Lance picks his nose and deposits his bogey under the table. I may be a bit overweight but he's actually repulsive.

'An uncle of mine,' admits Axel, after a short pause. 'Fred Pink.'

'Fred Pink's your *uncle*?' Angelica gawps. 'No shit! The window cleaner in the coma? But you're a Hardwick, not a Pink.'

'Fred Pink's my mother's brother. My mother is Hardwick née Pink. Slade Alley is Fred's obsession, I'm sorry to say.'

'Why "sorry"?' asks Fern, the question I wanted to ask.

Axel wrinkles his mouth. 'Uncle Fred feels . . . Oh, "chosen".'

'Chosen for what?' presses Fern. 'By whom?'

Axel shrugs. 'Chosen to find out the truth about Slade House. He had a hard time adjusting to real life after his nine years in a coma, and he's, uh, in care now. Out beyond Slough. In a . . . unit.'

'Too bloody brilliant,' declares Lance, holding up a palm to indicate he's about to belch; and he belches. 'All the supernatural yarns need a realist explanation *and* a supernatural one. Like, is the hero *really* seeing ghosts, or is he having a thermonuclear breakdown? I *love* this case. I'm in, Ax.'

'The more the merrier,' says Axel, unmerrily.

Angelica sips her pale ale. 'It's an intriguing case study – but how are the six of us s'posed to find this Slade House and all these missing people when like a ga*zill*ion cops failed?'

'The question's not how,' says Axel, 'it's when. Look at the dates, people.' He taps the A4 sheet. 'Use your grey matter.'

I look again, but all I see are the man, woman and boy staring out of their inky Xeroxed images. Little did they know. My fingers find the jade pendant that arrived from my sister in New York this morning. It's a symbol of eternity and I love it.

Todd the mathematician works it out first. 'Christ, I've got it. The Bishops vanished on the last Saturday in October 1979; fast-forward nine years, and Gordon Edmonds vanishes on the last Saturday in October 1988; fast-forward *anoth*er nine years, and you get . . .' He glances at Axel, who nods. 'Today.'

'Last Saturday in October 1997,' says Lance. 'Shitting scoobies, Axel. Today. Today!' Lance is able to take the piss and be sincere all at once. 'A mystery house that only blinks into existence one night every nine years. God, I've got a hard-on as big as Berkshire. Drink up!'

Westwood Road's street lamps have orange haloes of fine drizzle. Cars dash from speed bump to speed bump. A St John ambulance trundles past us, not in a hurry. The guys lead the way, with Lance airing a theory that Slade House could be the mouth of a miniature black hole. I'd love to add something that would make Todd respect me as a sharp thinker, but I'm always too slow. Angelica and Fern are arguing about whether or not *When Harry Met Sally* is offensive to women, which leaves me bringing up the rear. My customary place. I look at the rooms with undrawn curtains and see sofas, lamps, pictures, and look – a girl practising the piano in a room as blue as July. She has short hair, a blue and grey school uniform, and let's call her Grace. Grace looks upset because she can't get her piano piece just perfect, but as her elder sister I'd be a gifted pianist and I'd help Grace out. I'd never tell her, 'You'd feel better about yourself if you lost a few pounds.' Mum's making dinner in the back, not for a dozen bitchy Shell Oil wives but just for Dad, Grace, me and Freya, who didn't jet off to New York as soon as she graduated, but who works in London so she can hang out with me every weekend. Mum's not cooking fusion, demi-veg or faddish, she's cooking roast chicken with potatoes, carrots and gravy. I'm stirring the gravy. Dad's walking home from the station because he's not a £190k-a-year-plus-share-options oil exec – he works for Greenpeace, but only for £40k. Okay, £60k. Grace senses me watching, looks up and out at the street, and I do a little wave, but she draws the curtain. You never know if they've seen you.

'Are you okay, Sally?' Jesus, it's Todd. Standing right next to me.

'Yes,' I say, jolted into acting normal. 'Yes, I . . .'

The others are watching me and waiting.

'Sorry everyone, I was, uh . . .'

'Away with the fairies?' suggests Fern, not unkindly.

'Maybe,' I admit, 'but I'm back again now.'

'Wagons roll, then,' says Lance and we're off, but Todd stays by me. He's got a baggy duffel coat and there's room in his pockets for both our hands. Telepathically I tell Todd, *Take my hand*, but he doesn't. Why is it only slime-balls like Lance who hit on me? If I were slimmer, and funnier, and sexier, I'd know what to say to Todd now so before we even found Slade Alley Todd'd be telling me, 'Look, Sal, I vote we grab ourselves a Chinese takeout and then head back to my place for coffee,' and I'd reply, 'You know, I vote we forget the takeout.' We step aside for an Afghan hound trailing a woman in a long coat and sunglasses. She ignores us. I mutter, 'Charmed, I'm sure.'

Todd makes a 'Mm' noise to show me he's on my side.

We walk a few paces. There's something invisible connecting us. I hear a grunting noise like sex getting louder and louder but it's only a jogger running by. He's wearing black and glow-in-the-dark orange like he's escaped from an acid rave somewhere.

'Sal,' says Todd. 'I don't want to sound too forward—'

'No, not at all,' I answer nervously, and my heart goes zoom. 'It's fine. Of course. Yes.' He pauses, confused: 'But I haven't asked you yet.'

Sally Timms, you stupid oink. 'I just meant "Ask away!"'

'People, I've found it!' Lance calls out, a few paces ahead, and the moment's gone and my heart goes 'No!'. Todd shines his torch up at an easy-to-miss plaque: SLADE ALLEY. The passageway's dark and narrow, only a bit wider than a pushchair. Lance says, 'Spooky as hell, or what?'

'Of course it's spooky,' says Fern, lighting one of her French cigarettes. 'It's nearly night, and it's an enclosed space.'

'*I* feel,' says Angelica in a wavery voice, 'presences here.'

One part of me thinks, *Yeah, yeah, sure you do*, but another part of me kind of . . . knows what Angelica means, actually. Slade Alley cuts through black shadow before turning sharp left under a feeble lamp that pulses dimly. If I was a 'presence', this is the kind of place I'd be drawn to.

'Who'll disturb the presences first?' asks Lance, deadpan.

'You'd be less cocky,' says Angelica, 'if *you* had the Sight.'

'Fred's my uncle,' says Axel, 'so I'll lead the way. Ready?'

Lance, Angelica, Fern, me and Todd follow Axel, in that order. I feel safe with Todd behind me, and trail my gloved fingers along the bricks on each side; Slade Alley can't be more than three feet across. A *properly* fat person – fatter than me, I mean – couldn't get past someone coming the other way. 'It's cold,' I murmur to no one, but Todd hears: 'Sure is. The air's like a knife against your throat.'

'Cool echo,' says Lance. 'Balrogs of the deep, I summon thee!'

'Mind who you're invoking,' says Angelica, school-marmishly.

Lance bursts into an echoey recital of 'Bohemian Rhapsody' before Axel tells him, 'Put a cork in it, Lance.' He's reached the corner under the lamp, and seconds later the six of us are huddled there. After the left turn, Slade Alley runs on for forty or fifty paces – it's hard to see – until it turns right under another high-up, flickery lamp. 'Always a bad sign,' says Lance, 'those buzzing bulbs. Anyone seen *Candyman*?' I actually have but I don't say so and nobody else says anything either. Slade Alley's just an alley in an ordinary town, but its brick walls are as high as two men and block any view of anything. The sky's just a long strip of soupy dusk over our heads. My back's pressed against Todd, who smells of damp wool, warmth and mint. First chance I get, I'll ask him what he was about to ask me back on the street. Then he'll pluck up the courage to ask me out. I have to make this happen, to take control for once. 'No sign of a gate,' says Lance. 'It's just one long wall.'

'Two long walls, you'll find,' says Angelica, annoyingly.

'Okay,' says Axel. 'This alley may be a POS.'

'What's a POS when it's at home?' asks Lance.

'Paranormal Occurrence Site, which explains why Angelica's picking up presences.' God, Angelica looks *so* pleased with herself. 'Lance, Fern, Todd: I need you to scan the right-hand wall, every square inch. All the way to the far end. Angelica, Sally and I'll take the left. We're looking for PAIs. Which is an abbreviation of – anyone?'

Todd clears his throat: 'Psychic Anomaly Indicators.'

'Excellent,' says Axel, and I kind of feel pleased too.

'Remind me what a PAI looks like, exactly,' says Fern.

'Items, signs, writing,' says Axel. 'They manifest themselves in many different forms. Anything that's out of place could be a PAI.'

'I'll search for rips in the membrane,' says Angelica.

'What membrane?' asks Fern, just as Angelica hoped.

'The membrane between worlds. You can't see it, though. It's only visible to empaths. Those of us with developed chakra vision.'

'Ah, of course,' says Fern, as if she's profoundly impressed. '*That* membrane.'

'Open-mindedness is a wonderful thing,' says Angelica. 'Try it sometime.'

Fern lights another cigarette. 'If you're too open-minded, your brain falls out.' I can't see Angelica's face in the shadows, but I'm pretty sure she'll be firing death-rays at Fern. 'Not sure if this is a PAI,' Lance calls out a few yards ahead. 'But it *is* a gate.' Everyone joins Lance, who crouches next to a small black iron door. At least, I think it's a door. It's low and very narrow, like it was built for skinny hobbits, but it's got no handle or latch or sign or anything.

'PAIs are often camouflaged as normal objects,' says Axel.

'Looks solid.' Fern raps her knuckles on it. 'Feels solid.'

'Don't knock!' Angelica tells Fern. 'You may wake a hostile entity.' She presses her palm against it. 'Emanations. Definitely.'

'Odd that none of us noticed it from the corner,' I say.

'It's a narrow door,' says Fern. 'From an obtuse angle.'

'No keyhole,' says Lance. 'The lock must be inside.' He presses the doorframe at various points.

'What's that in aid of?' asks Angelica.

'Release latches.' But the door stays shut. 'If I stood on your shoulders,' Lance says to Axel, 'I might *just* be able—'

'Not before my skeleton collapsed.' Axel turns to Fern – not to lardy-arsed Sally Timms, obviously. 'Fern, could you climb—'

'Forget it,' says Fern. 'If Slade House *is* on the other side of this wall, this titchy door can't be the only way in. Why don't we just follow the alley out to the street and walk round the other side until we reach the main gates?'

This makes a lot of sense, but Lance isn't having it. 'Ah, but if it was that simple, the police would have found it, yeah? Interdimensional wormholes don't have "other sides" or "main gates". This is the door all right.' There's something mocking about how Lance says this, and a voice in my head says, *Don't trust him, he's toying with all of you.*

Then something strange happens: my hand decides to press itself hard against the door, and a zap of heat goes through my palm. I let out a yelp of surprise like a trodden-on puppy and the small black iron door opens. Like it was only waiting to be asked. It waits, ajar . . .

'Bugger me,' says Lance. 'Not literally, Axel.'

'Looks like Sal's got the magic touch,' says Todd.

'It was probably open the whole time,' says Angelica, but I'm so spooked, I don't even care.

We emerge from a shrubbery and stare up a long lawn at a big old stone house. A Virginia creeper, dark crimson in the twilight, grows up one side. Faint stars shine through the gaps in the cloud but the sky's still a little lighter and the air's a little warmer than it was in the alley. 'Viewed through my non-psychic eyeballs,' says Fern, 'Slade House looks more *Rocky Horror Picture Show* than "a membrane between worlds".' Angelica can't rise to the bait because Fern's right. We are looking at a student house, mid-Hallowe'en party. 'Novocaine for the Soul' by Eels thumps out, Bill Clinton and a nun are canoodling on a bench, and a gorilla, a Grim Reaper and a Wicked Witch of the West are sitting around a sundial thing, smoking. 'My, my, you're a crafty one, Axel,' says Lance.

'Huh?' asks Axel, vaguely; then, sharply, '"Crafty"?'

'You've lured your poor disciples to a piss-up, right?'

'I'm not luring anyone anywhere,' snaps Axel.

'Hang on,' says Fern. 'Is this the same Slade House that the collective brain of the Thames Valley Police failed to locate?'

Axel mumbles, 'Apparently so, but . . .' His 'but' fizzles out.

'Good,' says Fern. 'And while this fit of sanity lasts, could we rule out the theory that we just passed through a black hole?'

'Fern?' It's the Wicked Witch of the West, walking over. 'Fern! I thought it was you!' The witch is American and her mask is green. 'We met at Professor Marvin's seminar on Jacobean drama. Kate Childs, Blithewood College exchange student. Though right now,' she gives a twirl, 'I'm moonlighting for the forces of evil. Gotta say, Fern, your performance in *The Monkey's Paw* blew – me – away.'

'Kate!' Fern the future A-lister forgets us, her embarrassing tagger-alongers. 'So glad you gave a monkey's about *Monkey's*.'

'You kidding?' Kate Childs takes a long drag on her spliff and releases a plume of dope smoke. 'I literally died of envy.'

Lance asks, 'Are you smoking what I think you're smoking, you wicked *wick*ed worstest witch?'

'That depends,' the American girl gives Lance a dubious look, 'on what exactly it is you think I'm smoking.'

'Shut it a sec, Lance,' says Angelica. 'Excuse me – Kate. We'd just like you to settle something: is that building Slade House?'

Kate Childs smiles like it might be a trick question. 'Unless they've renamed it in, like, the last half hour: yes.'

'Thank you,' Angelica continues. 'And who lives here?'

'Me and about fifteen Erasmus exchange scholars. You guys *are* here for the Hallowe'en party, right?'

'Definitely,' says Lance. 'We're six psychic investigators.'

'So just to be clear,' says Angelica, 'the university owns Slade House, this building, where you live?'

'Technically, the Erasmus Institute owns it, though a university groundsman mows the grounds on his shit-on mower. There's a sign round the front that— Christ, did I just say "shit-on mower"? I did, didn't I?' Kate Childs bends over with silent laughter, which vanishes as quickly as it came. 'Sorry. What were we saying?'

'The sign,' says Axel. 'The sign round the front.'

'"Slade House, Erasmus Scholarship Centre, Sponsoring Cross-Cultural Understanding in Education since 1982." Walk past it every day. It's by the –' she jabs a finger over the roof of Slade House '– big gates. So if *that*'s all settled . . .' Kate Childs points to the big house. 'Eat, drink, be merry: tomorrow we . . .' She waves her hand to shake out the last verb, but gives up and offers Lance her spliff.

Lance turns to us. 'I'll see *you* guys later.'

'I'll lodge a formal apology on ParaSoc's records,' says Axel, as he, Angelica, Fern, Todd and me approach the house. 'My uncle swore that Slade House had never been found.' Axel slaps the stone wall of the building. 'Either he's a liar or he's delusional. Who cares? My first error was to believe him.'

I feel bad for Axel. 'He's your uncle. You shouldn't feel guilty just for believing him.'

'Sal's right,' says Todd. 'No harm's been done.'

Axel ignores us. 'My second error was a failure to reconnoitre the locale. A short stroll down Cranbury Avenue would have done the job. It was unforgivable.' Axel's near tears. 'Cavalier. Amateurish.'

'Who cares?' says Fern. 'Looks like a slinky humdinger of a party.'

Axel adjusts his scarf. 'I care. ParaSoc is suspended until further notice. Goodnight.' With that, he walks down the passage around the side of Slade House.

'Axel,' Angelica rushes after him, 'hold your horses . . .'

Todd watches them disappear. 'Poor guy.'

'Poor Angelica,' says Fern, which I don't understand; I thought Fern hated her. 'Well, when in Rome . . .' She trots up the steps and slips inside. Todd turns to me and makes a *What a night!* face. I make a *Tell me about it!* face. He readjusts his glasses. If I were his girlfriend I'd make him get frameless ones to let his doomed–poet good looks shine. 'Todd, you wanted to ask me something.'

Todd looks all hunted. 'Did I?'

'Earlier. On the street. Before Lance found the alley.'

Todd scratches his neck. 'Did I? I . . .' I deflate. Todd's pretending to have forgotten because he's got cold feet. It's all these waif-thin girls gyrating their skinny bodies around. 'Maybe if we go inside and chat, Sal,' Todd's saying, 'it'll come back to me. I – I mean, if you've got no other plans tonight. A quick drink and a chat. No strings attached.'

'Just the one sister,' I tell Todd a second time, louder, because 'Caught by the Fuzz' by Supergrass is pumping on the stereo. We're huddled in a corner by an oven with a noisy fan. The kitchen's crammed, misty with cigarette smoke and smells of bins. Todd's drinking a Tiger beer from a bottle and I'm drinking shit red wine from a plastic cup.

'Your sister's older than you, I'm guessing,' says Todd.

'Was it a fifty-fifty guess, or can you really tell?'

'An eighty-twenty hunch. What's her name?'

'Freya. She lives in New York these days.'

Laughter explodes nearby; Todd cups his ear: 'Wassat?'

'Freya. As in the kick-ass Norse goddess of . . . um . . .'

'Love, sex, beauty, fertility, gold, war and death.'

'That's the one,' I say. 'As opposed to "Sally", a doomed pit pony, or a tart in the East End docks in a Dickens novel.'

'Not true!' Todd actually looks hurt. 'Sally's a sunny name. It's kind.'

'All the research suggests that Freyas go *way* farther in life than Sallys. Name me *one* famous Sally. Go on. You can't, can you? My sister won every medal going at school; picked up good Mandarin in Singapore, fluent French in Geneva; graduated in journalism from Imperial College this June; moved in with her boyfriend in Brooklyn, who is of course a hotshot Chinese-American documentary maker;

and got a job with a photo agency on Bleecker Street. Not an internship – an actual paid job. All within a fortnight of touching down at JFK. That's *so* Freya. If I sound jealous, I am. God, Todd, did you spike my wine with truth serum?'

'No, but don't stop, Sal. I love hearing you talk.'

I actually heard him perfectly well but I love hearing Todd using the words 'I', 'love' and 'you' in such close proximity so I ask him, 'Say that again?'

'I said, I love hearing you talk. Maybe Freya's jealous of you, too.'

'As if! Here's *my* potted biography, to prove the point: Sally Timms, born Canterbury in 1979.' Todd's paying close attention, like he really wants to hear this. 'Dad was a Shell Oil man and Mum was a Shell Oil wife. They still are – Shell's like Hotel California: you can check out but you can never leave. Dad got promoted to the Singapore office when I was eight, and we all moved out. Singapore's all rules, every square yard's hemmed in. When I was twelve, I had a, kind of . . . breakdown, and . . .' I hesitate, wondering if Todd's admiring my honesty or thinking, *Headcase, headcase, pull back, pull back*; but his beautiful brown eyes encourage me to carry on. 'My parents decided I wasn't culturally adaptable, so I ended up at a girls' school in Great Malvern, in Worcestershire. Six years of English weather; of crap English food; lots of Singaporean girls, ironically; lots of rich people's problem daughters, too. Like me.' *But slimmer, prettier and bitchier.* 'I should've fitted right in, but I . . . Actually, I loathed it.'

Todd asks, 'Did your parents know you were so unhappy?'

I shrug. 'It was a matter of making my bed and lying in it. Dad got promoted to Brunei, Mum stayed in Singapore, Freya left for Sydney – this was all pre-email, of course, so we all had to . . . to build our own lives, pretty much independently. We reconvened for summers and Christmases, but while Mum and Freya were like long-lost sisters, I was the . . . well, I'd like to say "black sheep of the family", but black sheep are kind of cool. Todd, I can't be*lieve* you want to listen to me whinge on.'

'You're not whingeing. You had a tough time.'

I sip my shit wine. 'Not compared to an AIDS orphan or any North Korean or a Shell Oil wife's maid. I forget my good luck.'

'Who doesn't?' says Todd, and I'm about to say, 'You don't, I bet,' but then this black guy with hair dyed white opens the oven door next to us: ''Scuse us, 'scuse us, boys 'n' girls.' He slides out a tray of garlic bread and offers us a slice: 'G'arn, g'arn – ya know ya want to.' I don't know if it's a real London accent or a Cockney piss-take, but the garlic bread smells authentically gorgeous. I hesitate. Todd says, 'I will if you will.'

'Mum's blind,' Todd tells me when we're on our third slice.

Actually I'm on my fourth, but I stop chewing. 'Todd.'

'Hey, it's no big deal. People live with worse.'

'It's not *not* a big deal. Is that why you live at home?'

'Uh-huh. I got accepted at Edinburgh, and Mum and

Dad were all, "Go on, son, it's your life," but Dad's not getting any younger, I'm an only child, so I stayed. I don't regret it. I've got my own granny flat above the garage, all mod cons, for' – Todd realises that if he says 'girlfriends' it'll look like he's hitting on me – 'for, uh . . .'

'Personal space and independent living?' I offer, wiping a dribble of butter off my chin as sophisticatedly as possible.

'Personal space and independent living. Can I use that?'

I dare to say, 'Only with me.' I try not to ogle as Todd grins and licks garlic butter off his fingers. 'If it's not too personal, Todd, can I ask if your mum was born blind or if it came on in later life?'

'Later life. She was diagnosed when I was eleven. Retinitis pigmentosa, or RP to its friends. She went from about 90 per cent vision to less than 10 per cent in a year. Not the best of times. These days she can tell if it's night or day, and that's about it. But we're still lucky. Sometimes RP ushers in deafness and chronic fatigue as well, but Mum can hear me swear from a mile away. She works, too, transcribing audiobooks into Braille. She did that Crispin Hershey novel *Desiccated Embryos*.'

I say, 'Cool,' but don't add that I thought the book was massively overrated. Todd's knee's almost touching mine. If I were drunker, or Fern, or Freya, I'd put my hand on it and tell Todd, 'Kiss me, you idiot, can't you see I want you to?' and I'd sound so classy. But if I tried it, I'd come over like a drunk podgy sad-sack slut – like a female Lance – and I can't, won't, mustn't, don't. 'Cool.'

'You and Mum'd get on.' Todd stands up. 'Really well.'

Was that an invitation? 'I'd *love* that, Todd,' I say, inserting 'I', 'love' and 'Todd' into the same sentence. 'God, I'd *love* to meet her.'

'Let's make it happen. Look, I'm going to track down the bathroom. Promise not to go anywhere?'

'I do. Most solemnly.' I watch him vanish among the bodies. Todd Cosgrove. A good name for a boyfriend. 'Todd' is kind of classless while 'Cosgrove' is borderline posh. Nice balance. 'Sally Timms' sounds like a shat-upon events organiser, but 'Sal Cosgrove' could be a rising star at the BBC, or an interior designer to the stars, or a legendary editor. Sal Cosgrove isn't fat, either. She'd never wolf down a family-size bag of Minstrels and make herself vomit it up in the toilet afterwards. True, I only properly started talking with Todd half an hour ago, but every instance of undying love was only half an hour young, once upon a time.

Behind me, Darth Vader's slagging off his sociology lecturer to a thin-as-a-rake Incredible Hulk, while in front of me, the Grim Reaper's scythe slides to the floor as he, or she, flirts with a black angel with crumpled wings. I open my handbag and get out my Tiffany compact mirror – a 'sorry' present from Freya for being too busy for me to stay with her in New York in August. The girl in the mirror fixes her lipstick. With Todd as my official boyfriend, I'll stick to my diet, I'll only eat fruit for breakfast, I'll only eat half my present portions. Mum and Freya's jaws will drop when they see me. God, that'll feel good! So now that's decided, I walk over to the food counter. Popcorn, more garlic bread and two Wedgwood cake-stands piled high with brownies. One cake-stand has a little flag stuck into the topmost brownie, saying HASH BROWNIES, while the flag on the other one reads NO HASH BROWNIES. Apart from a Snickers bar before my Chaucer seminar, plus the tube of Pringles I had at the library, I haven't eaten a thing since lunch. If we gloss over the garlic bread. Plus, I burned skads of calories walking to The Fox and Hounds. One tiny no-hash brownie won't hurt . . .

. . . Holy hell, my mouth actually froths, they're that delicious. Dark chocolate, hazelnuts, rum and raisins. I'm about to eat a second one when this tanned blond blue-eyed Action Man body in muscle-hugging black appears and asks in a twenty-four-carat Aussie accent, 'Didn't we meet at the Morrissey gig?'

I would have remembered. 'Wrong girl, I'm afraid.'

'Story of my life. But seriously, you've got a doppel-gänger. I'm Mike – Melbourne Mike, as opposed to Margate Mike. Nice to meet you . . . Question Mark?'

We shake hands. 'I'm Sal,' I say, 'from Singapore, I suppose, if I'm from anywhere.' Singapore's more exotic than Malvern, as long as you've never actually lived there.

Melbourne Mike lifts a man-of-mystery eyebrow. 'Singapore Sal. I think I drank three of those one night in a cocktail bar. All on your ownsome, Sal?'

Of all the guys who've hit on me and who haven't

been drunk, which isn't actually all that many, Melbourne Mike's the best-looking by light years. But I've got Todd, so I give Mike an apologetic smile. "'Fraid not.'

Melbourne Mike does a courtly bow. 'Lucky bloke. Happy Hallowe'en.' Off he goes, and screw you, Isolde Delahunty at Great Malvern Beacon School for Girls and your platoon of body-fascist Barbies who spent eight years calling me 'Oink' like it was just a friendly nickname and saying, 'Oink oink, Oink!' when you passed me on the stairs or in the showers after hockey and I had to smile as if it were all just a funny joke but you *knew* it wasn't, you knew it was poison, so screw you Isolde Delahunty and screw all of you, wherever you are this evening, because I won, Oink just turned down a bronzed Australian surfer demigod, who now returns, still smiling, and points at the two cake-stands of brownies: 'By the way, Singapore Sal, some joker *may* have switched those signs over.'

I stop chewing. 'But that's really dangerous.'

'Some people, eh? Proper turd nuggets.'

At the foot of the stairs, a possibly Indian girl in an all-silver Tin Man costume reads my mind: 'Bathroom's this way, turn right, go along, it's there. Love the nail varnish, by the way. Peacock blue?' I get stuck between saying 'Yes' and 'Thanks' so it comes out 'Yanks'. Embarrassed, I follow her directions to a TV room where a bunch of guys are sitting on sofas watching *The Exorcist*, but I'm not staying for this. *The Exorcist* was on at the party in Malvern where I lost my virginity to a temporary best friend's ex-boyfriend's friend called Piers. Not a memory I cherish. Isolde Delahunty told the whole school about Oink Oink's Big Night, of course, and publicised what Piers had said about me afterwards. Now I'm in a blue-lit corridor booming with Björk's 'Hyperballad'. I pass a pair of tall doors and peer in. Thirty or so people are dancing in a big sort of ex-ballroom, lit by dim orange lamps. Some of the dancers are wearing stripped-down half-costumes, others are in only T-shirts or vests. I see Lance, sliding his hand over his own torso and neck. He tosses his dandruffy mane, spots me at the door and beckons me inside with a sex god's come-hither finger. I hurry off down the chilly corridor before I puke, round a corner, up some stairs and down some more until I find a bay window with a view of what might be the front of Slade House, with two big gateposts, though the streetlights and tree shadows and lines are blurred by mist and the fogged-up mullioned window, and to be honest I left my sense of direction in the kitchen. 'Hyperballad' has turned into Massive Attack's 'Safe from Harm'. Fern says my name. She's draped on a giant sofa in an alcove, French cigarette in one hand and a glass in the other, like she's doing a photo shoot. 'Hello. Are you enjoying the party?'

'Yes, actually. Have you seen Todd?'

'I've seen how besotted he is with *you*.'

I so, *so* badly want to hear this that I join her, just for a moment. The leather sofa's cold. I sink deep into it. It makes that dry squelchy noise like new snow or polystyrene that someone needs to invent a proper adjective for. 'Do you think so?'

'Big-time, Sal. It wasn't for paranormal experiences that Todd showed up tonight. When are you guys going to hook up? Tonight?'

I act cool, but I'm happier than I've been for . . . ever, actually. 'That depends. These things have their own pace.'

'Bollocks, girl.' Fern's cigarette hisses in her glass. 'You set the pace. Todd's a keeper. Lovely guy, really. Reminds me of my brother.'

Fern's never mentioned a brother – not that we've talked much. 'Is your brother a student, or an actor, or . . . ?'

'He's not anything these days. He's dead.'

'Oh God! I'm famous for my big mouth, Fern, I—'

'It's okay. It's fine. It happened, um . . . five Christmases ago. It's history.' Fern stares at the body of her cigarette bobbing in her drink.

I try to fix my blunder. 'Was it an accident? Or illness?'

'Suicide. Jonny drove his car over the edge of a cliff.'

'Bloody hell. I'm sorry. Why did he . . . I mean, no, forget it, it's not—'

'He didn't leave a note, but the cliff was a field away from the road to Trevadoe – our ancestral pile near Truro – so we know it wasn't an accident.' Fern acts a smile. 'He chose Daddy's vintage Aston Martin as his sarcophagus, too. The act *was* the suicide note, you might say.'

'I didn't mean to probe, Fern, I'm sorry, I'm an idiot, I—'

'Stop apologising! Jonny was the idiot. Well, that's not fair, Daddy had died two years before, Mummy had gone to pieces, so Jonny was juggling the legal mess, the death duties, a degree at Cambridge of course, *and* battling depression – unknown to us . . . His ideas about poker debts and honour, though, they really *were* idiotic – utterly, utterly idiotic. We could've just sold off an acre or two.' We watch the misted-up night through the misted-up window. 'That's why I joined ParaSoc, if I'm honest,' says Fern. 'If I could just see a ghost, just once – a Roman centurion or a headless horseman or, or Nathan and Rita Bishop, I'm not fussy . . . Just one ghost, so I *know* that death's not game over, but a door. A door with Jonny on the other side. Christ, Sally, I'd give *any*thing to know he didn't just . . . *stop*, that stupid afternoon. Anything. Seriously. Like' – Fern clicks her fingers – 'that.'

I unpeel my face off a big cold leather sofa in a dark alcove. 'Safe from Harm' is still on, so I can't have slept long. Fern's gone, but sitting a foot away is a guy dressed in a furry brown dressing gown and not a lot else, judging by his hairy legs and hairy chest. Right. He's not eyeing me up. Actually he's just staring at the blank wall – I thought there was a bay window there, but obviously not. The dressing-gown man's not that old, but he's going bald. He has sleepless owlish eyes and an almost-monobrow. Do I know him? Don't see how. It's strange that Fern would just vanish like that, straight after spilling her guts about her brother, but that's actresses for you. Maybe she was pissed off that I nodded off. I ought to find her and put it right. Poor Fern. Her poor brother. People are masks, with masks under those masks, and masks under those, and down you go. Todd must be back in the kitchen by now, but the sofa won't let me get up. 'Excuse me,' I ask Mr Dressing Gown, 'but do you know the way to the kitchen?'

Mr Dressing Gown acts like I'm not even there.

I tell him, 'Thanks, that's really helpful.'

His frown deepens, then, in slow motion, he opens his mouth. Is it supposed to be funny? His voice is dry as dust and he leaves big gaps between his words: 'Am . . . I . . . still . . . in . . . the . . . house?'

Jesus, he's stoned out of his Easter egg. 'Well, it's not Trafalgar Square, I can promise you that.'

More seconds pass. He's still talking to the blank wall. It's bloody weird. 'They . . . took . . . a . . . way . . . my . . . name.'

I humour him: 'I'm sure you'll find it again in the morning.'

The man looks towards me, but not at me, as if he can't quite place where my words are coming from. 'They . . . don't . . . e . . . ven . . . let . . . you . . . die . . . pro . . . per . . . ly.'

So far, so loony tunes. 'Whatever you've been smoking, I'd steer clear of it in future. Seriously.'

He cocks his shaved head and squints, as if hearing

words shouted from a long way off. 'Are . . . you . . . the
. . . next . . .'

I actually giggle; I can't help it. 'What, the next Messiah?'
The sofa vibrates to the giant bass in 'Safe from Harm'.
'Get a big strong black coffee,' I tell Mr Dressing Gown.
The man flinches, as if my words were pebbles hitting
his face. Now I feel bad about laughing at him. He screws
up his red eyes like he's trying to remember something.
'Guest,' he says, and blinks about him, Alzheimer's-ishly.
I wait for more, but there isn't any. 'Am I the next
guest? Is that what you're asking? The next guest?'
When the man speaks again he does this utterly
incredible ventriloquist's trick where he mouths his words
a second or two before you hear them. 'I . . . found . . . a
. . . wea . . . pon . . . in . . . the . . . cracks.'
His sound-delay trick's amazing, but his mention of
weapons triggers a warning light. 'Okay, thing is, I don't need
a weapon, so—' but from out of his dressing-gown pocket
the sad, half-naked stoner produces a short silver spike, about
six inches long. First I recoil in case it's a threat, but actually
he's offering it to me, like a gift. The non-spiky end's decorated with a fox's head, silver, small but chunky, with jewelled
eyes. 'It's lovely,' I'm saying, twizzling it. 'It looks antique. Is
it some kind of a, a geisha's hairpin or something?'

I'm alone on the leather sofa. Nobody's in the corridor.
Nobody's anywhere. Mr Dressing Gown's long gone, I sense,

but I'm still holding his fox hairpin. God, I zoned out again. This isn't a good habit. 'Safe from Harm' has turned into the Orb's 'Little Fluffy Clouds'. There was a blank wall here, I thought, but actually there's a small black iron door, exactly like the one in Slade Alley, only this one's already ajar. I go to it, crouch down, push it open and peer out, just my head. It's an alley. It looks very like Slade Alley, but it can't be because it can't be. My knees are still on the carpet, in Slade House. It's dark, with very high walls and no people. It's as quiet as the tomb. As they say. There's no 'Little Fluffy Clouds' out here; it's as if my head's passed through a sound-proof membrane. About fifty metres away to my left, the alley turns right under a flickery street lamp. To my right, about the same distance away, there's another lamp, another corner. It can't be Slade Alley. I'm in a corridor in the house, fifty, eighty, a hundred metres away – I'm no good with distances. So . . . drugs? Drugs. If one frickhead put hash into no-hash brownies, another frickhead-to-the-power-of-ten could have sprinkled something trippier in the punch-bowl. It happens. Two students Freya knew in Sydney went to Indonesia, ate some kind of stew with magic mushrooms in it, and thought they could swim home to Bondi Beach. One of them was rescued, but the body of the other was never found. What do you actually do if you find an impossible alleyway on an acid trip? Go down it? Could do. See if it takes me back to Westwood Road. But what about Todd, waiting for me, right now, in the kitchen, wondering where I am. No. I'd rather get back. Or . . .

Or . . .

What if Slade House is the hallucination, and this door's my way back? Not a rabbit hole into Wonderland but the rabbit hole home? What if—

Someone touches my back and I jerk back inside, into the corridor in Slade House, to the music, to the party, startled twice over to find the Wicked Witch of the West peering down. 'Hey, Sally Timms. You okay down there? You lost something?'

'Hi –' I search for her name '– Kate.'

'Are you feeling all right? Did you lose something?'

'No, no, I was just wondering where this door led to.'

The witch looks a bit puzzled. 'What door?'

'This door.' And I show Kate Childs – the blank wall. The doorless blank wall. I touch it. Solid. I get up, wondering how I bluff this, trying to buy time. My thoughts revolve. Yes, I'm hallucinating; yes, I ate or drank something with drugs in it; no, I can't handle telling Kate that someone's drugged me. 'Look, I'm sloping off home.'

'But the night's still so young, Sally Timms.'

'Sorry, it's this head cold. My period's started.'

Kate removes her knobbly Wicked Witch mask to show an anxious sisterly face framed by Barbie-blonde hair. 'Let me summon you a cab then. It's a genuine magic power I was born with. Click of the fingers.' She starts patting herself down like at airport security. 'I just happen to have an extremely handy state-of-the-art cellphone in one of these . . . witchy pockets.'

A taxi would be nice, but I've only got £2. 'I'll walk.'

She looks dubious. 'Is that such a great idea, if you're ill?'

'Positive, thanks. The fresh air'll do me good.'

The unmasked witch isn't sure. 'Why don't you ask Todd Cosgrove to get you home safe and sound? One of the last gentlemen in England, is Todd.'

I didn't know Kate knew Todd. 'Actually, I was just looking for him.'

'He's looking for you too, Sally. Up in the games room.'

Tonight feels like a board game co-designed by M. C. Escher on a bender and Stephen King in a fever. 'Which way's the games room?'

'The quickest way's back through the TV room, down the hall, up the stairs and keep climbing. You can't go wrong.'

Everyone's glued to the screen the way people are when something major's happened. I ask a half-turned werewolf what's happened. 'Some girl's been abducted, like.' The werewolf's a Northerner. He doesn't look at me. 'A student, a girl, from our uni.'

'Jesus. Abducted?'

'Aye, that's what they're saying.'

'What's her name?'

'Polly, or Sarah, or . . .' The werewolf's drunk. 'Annie?

She's only been missing five days, but a personal item was found, so now the police are afraid it's, like . . . a real kidnapping. Or worse.'

'What kind of personal item?'

'A mirror,' mumbles the werewolf. 'A make-up mirror. Hang on, look . . .' The TV shows our student union building, where a female reporter's holding a big pink microphone: 'Thank you, Bob, and here on the city campus tonight the mood can best be described as grim and sober. Earlier today the police issued an appeal for any information on the whereabouts of Sally Timms, an eighteen-year-old student last seen in the vicinity of Westwood Road on Saturday night . . .' The reporter's words all gloop together. Missing? Five days? Since Saturday? It's *still* Saturday! I've only been in Slade House for an hour. It must be another Sally Timms. But a photo of my face fills the screen and it's me, it's me, and the Sally Timms on the screen is wearing exactly, *exactly*, what I'm wearing now: my Zizzi Hikaru jacket and Freya's Maori jade necklace that arrived today. That I signed for at the porter's lodge only twelve hours ago. Who took that photo of me? When? How? The reporter thrusts her big pink microphone at Lance, *Lance Arnott*, who, apparently, is dancing in this building right now – while also speaking to a TV reporter two miles away, saying, 'Yeah, yeah, I saw her just before she disappeared, at the party, and—' Lance's cod-fish lips keep moving but my hearing kind of cuts out. I should be switching on the lights and shouting, 'NO NO NO, people, look, there's been some stupid mistake – *I'm*

Sally Timms, I'm here, it's okay!' but I'm afraid of the fuss, the shame, of being a spectacle, of being a news story, and I just can't. Meanwhile Lance Arnott's making a doubtful face: ''Fraid so, yeah. She had *serious* trouble adjusting to college life. Bit of a tragic figure: vulnerable, not very streetwise, know what I'm saying? There were rumours of drug use, dodgy boyfriends, that kind of stuff.' Now I'm angry, as well as frightened and confused as hell. How *dare* Lance say all that about me on live TV? For not fancying him, I'm a tragic, vulnerable druggie? The reporter turns back to the camera. 'A clear picture is emerging of the missing student as an unhappy girl; a loner, with weight issues; a girl who had trouble adjusting to real life after private schools in Singapore and Great Malvern. Following the discovery of her compact mirror in, uh,' the reporter shuffles her notes, 'Slade Alley earlier today, the friends and relatives of Sally Timms, while still hoping for the best, must, as the hours go by, be fearing the worst. This is Jessica Killingley, reporting live for *South Today*; and back to you in the studio, Bob.'

God knows what Freya, Mum and Dad must be thinking. Actually, I *know* what they're thinking: they're thinking I've been murdered. They urgently need to know I'm fine, the police need to call off the search, but I can't just announce it here. I pull back from the werewolf and bang into a sideboard. My hand touches something rubbery: a Miss Piggy mask. Thanks to Isolde Delahunty *et al* I've got bad associations with pigs, but if I don't put it on, any second now someone'll see me, point and shriek, so I just loop its cord round my head and cover my face. Cool. A bit of breathing space. What was the reporter saying about my compact mirror? I used it in the kitchen after Todd left. Didn't I? I check in my handbag . . .

. . . Gone. Normally I'd retrace my steps and hunt it down, but I want to get out of Slade House even more than I want Freya's gift back. She'll understand. She'll have to. Todd'll know what to do. Todd's unflappable. We'll slip away and sort out what needs to be sorted. Him and me.

At the foot of the stairs, a possibly Indian girl in an all-silver Tin Man costume says, 'Did you hear about Sally Timms, the missing girl?'

'Yes, I did.' I try to get by but she's blocking my path.

'Did you know Sally Timms well?' asks the Tin Man girl.

'Not very,' I answer, and slip by, up the stairs. The banister glides under my fingertips and the hubbub of the hallway fades away, like I'm climbing into a fog of silence. The carpet on the stairs is cream like margarine, the walls are panelled and hung with portraits, and up ahead is a small square landing, guarded by a grandfather clock. A pale carpet and an antique clock is asking for trouble in a student house, Erasmus scholars or not. The first picture shows a freckled girl; she's really lifelike. The next picture's of an old soldier with a waxed moustache, the sort who'd say, 'Roger wilco, chocks away'. I'm short of breath but

I can't have been climbing that long. I need to join a gym. Finally, I've reached the grandfather clock. Its face has no hands, only the words TIME IS, TIME WAS, TIME IS NOT. Highly metaphysical; deeply useless. To my left's a door, panelled, to match the walls. To my right, more stairs climb past more portraits to a pale door. Which is the games room? I knock on the panelled door.

I hear only the clock's rusty, oiled heart.

I knock again, but louder. Nothing . . .

. . . but the rhythmic grunt of cogs.

Turn the doorknob, then. Open the door. Just an inch. Peer in.

This room's igloo-shaped, lit by a bedside lamp, window-less, carpetless, and contains a large four-poster bed and not a lot else. The bed's maroon drapes are drawn. The mechanical grinding noise has stopped, but I call out softly, 'Todd?' in case he's in the bed. 'Todd? It's Sal.'

No reply, but if Todd ate a hash brownie – or actually a no-hash brownie – he might be asleep. Snoring softly, maybe, in that bed, like Goldilocks.

I'll just peep through the drape. That can't hurt.

Anyway, I'm unrecognisable in my Miss Piggy mask.

So I shuffle over the grainy floorboards and lift a flap of the velvet. Just an inch . . . 'Miss Piggy!' booms a man – Axel? – sweat-glazed in the blood-dim cocoon, and I only half block a shriek. The bed's taken up by a grotesque frame of naked limbs, chests, breasts, groins, shoulders, toes, buttocks, goitres and scrotums; an undrawable bone cage, a flesh loom, a game of Twister with several Siamese bodies pulled apart and smooshed together; up here's Angelica's head with her matted indigo hair and a tongue-stud showing; down there's Axel's head; in the core, I see their pneumatic sexes, swollen huge and crimson-raw like a Francis Bacon pornmare; the stink of bad fish is nause-ating and the Axel head grins at me through the slit in the drape, through my Miss Piggy eyehole, and he speaks, but his words are jolted out of him in Angelica's voice: 'Is – Oink – Oink – hun – gry – for – a – ba – con – sand – wich?' and the Angelica head, melded onto a flabby thigh with wrists where its ears should be, grunts back in Axel's voice, 'Don't – be – mean – Sal – ly – hates – it – when – we – call – her – that.'

I skitter back across the floor to the panelled door and slam it behind me, quivering with disgust, with horror, with . . . The grandfather clock is calm and collected. Far, far below, the black and white tiled hallway is quiet. Up above, the pale door's waiting. It's a bad acid trip. I've heard about them. Piers my first non-boyfriend had one once, and it sounded like this. Axel and Angelica were having sex, but I saw it through kaleidoscopic drug-tinted spectacles. I need to get Todd urgently so he can keep an eye on me. I walk up the stairs, past two portraits: one of a young rockabilly type with Brylcreemed hair and half-open shirt; the next, a woman with eyeliner like

Cleopatra and a beehive Martha and the Vandellas hairdo. The next portrait, however, stops me dead. It's of a boy in school uniform, and I've seen him once already tonight . . . I get out Axel's A4 sheet from my jacket and compare them. It's Nathan Bishop. My feet take me up to the next portrait, which shows Mr Dressing Gown from earlier. Now that Axel's case study is in front of me, I can name him: Gordon Edmonds. Who I spoke to, on the cold sofa, a little while ago. Or who I dreamed I spoke to. I don't know which. I don't even know if I'm *that* shocked to find Sally Timms staring out of the final picture, standing in her Zizzi Hikaru jacket with Freya's Maori pendant round her neck. The same image they used on TV. Except my eyes are now two freakish blanks, and she's frowning, as if I can't understand why I can't see any more, and as I watch, one of her index fingers rises to tap the inside face of the canvas . . . I half-huff half-shriek half-slip half-fall onto the ledge at the very top of the stairs, and my hand steadies me by shooting up and grasping the shiny doorknob on the pale door . . .

. . . which swings open and suddenly Todd's there looking at me, bloodless and thunderstruck. I say, 'Todd?' and he jumps back and I realise it's my mask so I yank it off and say his name again and Todd says, 'Sal, Sal, thank *Christ* I found you,' and now we're hugging. Todd's bony and skinny but his muscles are iron though he's really cold like he's just walked in from a frosty night. Behind him is the sloping ceiling of a dark attic. Todd uncouples himself from our hug and shuts the pale door. 'Something bad's happening in this house, Sal. We need to get out.'

We're both whispering. 'Yes, I know, someone's spiked our drinks. I'm seeing . . . impossible things. Like' – where do I begin? – 'Todd, the TV said I've been missing for *five days*. Missing! I can't be. And look –' I point at my eyeless portrait which has stopped moving now. 'It's me, that picture's me, wearing this' – I hold up the real necklace for Todd to see – 'which I only got today. It's insane.'

Todd swallows. 'I'm afraid it's worse than an acid trip, Sal.'

I see he's serious. I fumble at what it means. 'What, then?'

'We joined ParaSoc for paranormal experiences. We've found them. And they're not benign. They'll try to stop us getting out.'

I'm afraid to ask: 'Who'll try to stop us?'

Todd glances behind us at the pale door. 'Our hosts. The twins. I . . . put them to sleep, but they'll wake up soon. Angry and hungry.'

'Twins? What twins? What do they want?'

Todd says it low and level: 'To consume your soul.'

I wait for him to tell me he's joking. I wait. I wait.

Todd's holding my elbows. 'Slade House is their life-support machine, Sal, but it's powered by souls, and not just any old souls. It's like blood groups: the type they need is very rare, and your soul is that very rare type. We have to get you out. Now. We'll go down the stairs, out via the kitchen, across the garden, and once we're in Slade Alley, I think we'll be safe. Safer, anyway.'

I feel Todd's breath on my forehead. 'I saw some big gates onto Cranbury Avenue, and another black iron door in the hall.'

Todd shakes his head. 'That's wallpaper, to fool you. The one way out is the one way in: the aperture.'

'What about Fern, Lance, Axel, Angelica?'

A muscle in Todd's cheek twitches. 'They're beyond my help.'

'What do you mean? What'll happen to them?'

Todd hesitates. 'You're the fruit; they're the pith, stone and skin. They've been discarded.'

'But . . .' I point down the stairs – are there more stairs now? – to the square landing, but the door into the igloo room has gone. 'I – I saw Axel and Angelica . . . down there. Sort of.'

'You saw fleshy 3D Polaroids of Axel and Angelica which wouldn't stand much scrutiny close up. Listen.' Todd grips my hand. 'Carefully. On our way out, *speak to nobody*; respond to nobody; meet nobody's eye. Accept nothing, eat nothing, drink nothing. This version of Slade House is a shadow play, evoked into being. If you engage with it, the twins sense you; they'll wake; they'll extract your soul. Understand?'

Kind of. Yes. No. 'Who *are* you?'

'I'm a . . . a kind of bodyguard. Look, I'll explain back

at my parents' house. We *have* to go, Sal, or it'll be too late. Remember: vow of silence, eyes down, don't let go of my hand. I'll cloak us as best I can. Put that mask back on, too. It may sow a little extra confusion.'

Todd holds my hot hand in his cold one, and I focus on my feet to avoid looking at portraits. Time passes, steps fly under our feet, and we arrive at the grandfather clock. Its *krunk-kronk*s are all tempos all at once. The panelled door to the igloo room hasn't reappeared. 'There was a door here,' I whisper. 'Did I dream it?' Todd murmurs, 'Rats in a maze of moveable walls ask themselves the same thing.' Halfway down the lower flight of stairs, students start appearing in the hallway, chatting, arguing, smoking, flirting. The volume rises with every step. 'So you found him,' says the Tin Man girl with a smile, pressing a black drink against her silver cheek. 'I'm Urvashi. What's your name?' Todd squeezes my hand to warn me against answering. It's like the Don't Say Yes or No game Dad used to play with me and Freya on car journeys, but here you mustn't be tricked into saying anything at all. Urvashi the Tin Man's in my face: 'Oy, Miss Piggy! Answer, or you'll be Miss Piggy for the rest of forever! Hey!' But Todd pulls me on, and Urvashi's lost in a blur of faces, masks, bodies, and soon we're back in the kitchen. 'Caught by the Fuzz' by Supergrass is pumping out of a stereo. Todd leads me around the edge and it's going well until we pass within inches of Todd Cosgrove and Sally Timms, huddled in a corner by an oven with a noisy fan. I stop. Fake Todd's drinking Indian beer from a bottle and Fake Me's drinking shit red wine from a plastic cup. Fake Todd's saying, 'Your sister's older than you, I'm guessing,' and Fake Sally nods. 'Was it a fifty-fifty guess, or can you really tell?' I hear Todd − Real Todd − inside my ear canal telling me, *Keep going, Sal, they're flypaper.* He propels me on, his arm round my waist, past a table of bottles, cans, a punchbowl and two Wedgwood cake-stands full of brownies. We go under an archway into a utility room with a dozen people between us and the door, including a dug-up corpse, an unravelling mummy, a tube of Colgate toothpaste with a red bucket for a cap and Lance Arnott who blocks my way, looking like a lost soul in an old painting of hell: 'There's something evil in here!' *It's not him,* says Todd in my inner ear, but Lance is gripping my lapels: it *is* him, I smell his yeasty BO. 'Please, Sal, I know I was an arsehole, but please don't leave me! Please!'

'Okay, okay,' I whisper, 'we'll take you with us.'

Instantly, Lance's face dribbles off, revealing something bonier, hungrier and toothier beneath. I try to scream but my throat's locked. Todd steps between us and traces signs onto the air − I half see the living black lines he inscribes before they vanish − and then the thing who wore the Lance Arnott disguise flickers off and on and off . . . and is gone.

I gasp, 'What the f—'

I unplugged the modem, Todd tells me − telepathically, I

notice a moment later, and instantly accept. *But the twins are waking.* The kitchen's silent.

My heart's drumming and a vein in my neck's twitching in time. Some of the partygoers are turning our way, sensing that we don't belong. *Act normally*, says Todd's voice, *don't show fear*, and he leads me to the back door. Locked. Not showing fear's one thing, but I feel it. It's slithering around my body, just under my skin. Todd makes a threading motion with his fingers and the door opens. He bundles us through. *I'll lock them in behind us*, Todd tells me, and turns to trace a symbol at the door. It's dark out. Down the garden, I make out the Slade Alley wall behind the shrubbery, just. Fern Penhaligon appears, looking delighted. 'Sal, you left this on the sofa – catch!' She tosses me my Tiffany compact, the gift from Freya, and I catch it—

Dark fireworks zigzagged over marbled skies; the zigzags plucked at harpsichord wires and I floated on the Dead Sea, and could've stayed there forever, but a wave of pain lifted me up, high as spires, then hurled me down hard onto the pebbles at the foot of Slade House. Todd's scared face appears up close. 'Sal! Can you hear me? Sal!' My skin pops like bubble wrap and I grunt a yes. 'The orison's imploding – can you walk?' Before I can answer, Todd hauls me upright and my legs are heavy and bendy and I step on something snappable – my Tiffany mirror – and we stagger across the upper lawn. We reach a wisteria trellis where a creeping shockwave catches us and bowls us over a cropped lawn covered with tiny fan-shaped leaves. I want to lie there forever, but Todd drags me up again, and Slade House by night's shimmering fat and thin, reflected or refracted. Then figures come strolling through the shimmer. Rows and clusters of figures, ambling like they know they don't have to hurry. Their bodies are blurs but there's Axel's face; there's Angelica; everyone in my Chaucer seminar; my teachers from Great Malvern; Isolde Delahunty and her Barbies; Mum, Dad, Freya. Todd pulls me. '*Run*, Sal!' And we try, God we try, but it's like running through water; rose-thorns scratch my eyes; a bucking path trips us; damson trees claw us; and a shrubbery billows up and its roots try to hook our ankles, but here's the small black iron door. Stupidly, I look back, like you never should in stories. The figures flicker nearer. There's Piers, who said his night with Oink'd been like shagging a dead blubber whale on a beach, only smellier.

Todd's saying to me: 'You have to open the aperture, Sal.'
He means the black iron door. How? 'What do I do?'
'Open it, like you did before! I can't do it.'
The faceless walkers are closing in.
I'm shaking. 'What did I do before?'
'You pressed it. With your palm!'
So I press the small black iron door –
– and it presses back, just as hard.
'Why isn't it working?'
'You're too scared, it's blocking your voltage.'
I look behind us. Yards away. They've got us.

Todd begs: 'Forget the fear, Sal. *Please.*'

'I can't!'

'You *can.*'

'I *can't!*'

Todd presses his hands against my cheeks and gently, firmly, kisses my lips and whispers, 'Please, Sal.' I'm still scared, but something's unlocked, and something flows through my hand, the door swings open and Todd's pushing me through into . . .

. . . a starless, bodiless, painless, timeless blackness. I don't know how long I've been here. Minutes, years, I just don't know. I passed through a phase when I thought I must be dead, but my mind's alive, even if I can't tell if I'm in my body or not. I prayed to God for help, or just for a light, apologising for not believing in him and trying hard not to think about what a sociopathic bigot He is in the Old Testament and the Book of Revelation, but no reply came. I thought about Freya and Mum and Dad, and tried and failed to remember the last things I'd said to them. I thought about Todd. If he'd survived, he'd be helping the police look for me, even though I doubted this was a place where sniffer dogs could track you. I hoped Todd wasn't angry at me for interacting with Fake Fern and catching the mirror. Was that a fatal mistake, like Orpheus looking back? A dirty trick, if so. My hands just acted on reflex to save my mirror. But legends and stories are as full of dirty tricks as life is and however much time has gone by, nothing has changed, and all I have are memories – the brightest of them all being Todd's hurried kiss – to keep me company and to keep me sane in the starless, bodiless, painless, timeless blackness.

After minutes or months, a dim dot of light appears. I was afraid I'd gone blind, like Todd's mum. Seconds or years later, the dot grows into a slit of flame, the flame of a candle, a candle on a strange candlestick that sits in front of me, on the bare floorboards. The flame's absolutely still. It's not bright enough to reveal much of the room – an attic? – but by its light I see three faces. To my right sits Kate Childs, the Wicked Witch of the West, dressed in a grey Arab-style cloak thing, but now in her mid-thirties. Have I really been here so long? Have all those years been stolen from me? To my left hovers another vaguely familiar face . . . Jesus, it's Melbourne Mike. He's now the same age as the older Kate Childs, too, also motionless and Buddha-posed, and also wearing an ash-grey robe. Now I see them both in the same field of vision, I realise they're twins. The third face is Miss Piggy, watching me over the candle, about six paces dead ahead. Or rather, a kneeling girl in a Miss Piggy mask. A girl wearing a Zizzi Hikaru jacket with a Maori pendant round her chubby neck. Me, or my reflection. I try to move, speak, or even grunt, but my body won't respond. My brain works, my eyes work, that's about it. Like that Frenchman in the book Freya sent me, *The Diving Bell and the Butterfly* . . . locked-in syndrome, it's called. But the French guy could blink one eyelid, that's how he managed to communicate. I can't even do that. Left of the mirror is a pale door with a gold doorknob. A memory of that same door from an earlier time drags itself into focus . . . the room at the top of Slade House. The 'games room'. Have the three of us been drugged and brought here? Who by? And where's Todd?

'The Cosgrove boy's been let go, with the other waifs and strays you brought in with you,' Kate Childs says. The candle flame quivers. Her American accent's gone, replaced by crisp, upper-class English, not unlike my mother's. 'You're here in Slade House at my and my brother's behest. I'm Norah, and this is Jonah.'

I try to ask, *What do you mean,* 'The Cosgrove boy's been let go'*?* but my mouth isn't working, not even a little bit.

'Dead. He didn't suffer. Don't mourn. He never loved you. Over the last few weeks, culminating in tonight's show, he was my brother's ventriloquist's dummy, mouthing all those lovey-dovey lies you yearned so badly to hear.'

I try to tell this Norah she's insane, that I *know* Todd loves me.

'You tell her,' Norah orders Melbourne Mike – or Jonah – irritably, 'or she'll taste all saccharine and powdery.'

Jonah, if that's his actual name, sneers my way. 'It's all true, sweetie. Every word.' His Australian accent's gone; he has a plummy public school voice. 'I was inside Todd Cosgrove's head and I promise you, he found Sally Timms as erotic as a tub of lard forgotten at the back of the fridge.'

You're lying! Todd kissed me. Todd tried to help me escape.

'Let me translate it into Stupidest Oink Oink. Everything from the pub to the aperture in Slade Alley was real. This attic is real, too, and these are our real bodies. Between the iron door and waking up here, however, was an orison: a live, 3D stage set, projected from inside this lacuna in time,' Jonah drums on the floorboards, 'by my outrageously gifted sister. A scripted vision. I was in it too, or strictly speaking my soul was there, moving Todd's body, saying Todd's lines, but everything else – the people you met, the rooms you passed through, the tastes you tasted – was a local reality brought into being by my sister. Your and Todd's thrilling bid for freedom was another part of the rat's maze we had you run through, an orison inside an orison. A sub-orison. We need a better name for it, I agree. I'd ask you to help us to think of one, but you're dying.'

My stubborn Me insists, *You're lying, this is all a bad acid trip.*

'No,' Jonah sounds pleased, 'you're really dying. Your respiratory system. No muscles. Think about it. Is that the bad acid trip too?'

To my horror, I realise he's right. My lungs aren't working. I can't gasp, or fall over, or do anything but kneel here and slowly suffocate. The twins now appear to lose interest in me. 'I am speechless with admiration, Sister,' Jonah's saying.

'You haven't been speechless for a hundred years,' says Norah.

'If the academy awarded Oscars for Best Orison, you'd be a shoo-in. Truly, it was a masterpiece. Cubist, post-modern – superlatives fail me.'

'Yes yes yes, we're geniuses – but what about the policeman? His residue was substantial enough to *speak* with the guest. And the aperture – appearing of its own accord like that, and open. The girl nearly bolted.'

'Ah, but she didn't bolt – and why? Cupid's noose was firmly round her neck is why. Todd Cosgrove was a trickier role to pull off than Chloe Chetwynd, you'll concede. Plod would've mounted a gashed slab of raw liver, while this little piggy needed proper wooing.'

These words would normally draw blood, but right now I'm worrying about how long you can survive without oxygen. Three minutes?

Norah Grayer twists her head as if screwing it into a socket. 'As per usual, Brother, you're missing the point. With each Open Day, these aberrations grow worse.'

Jonah flexes his spidery fingers. 'As per usual, Sister, you're spouting paranoid nonsense. Once again, dinner is served without hitch or hiccup. Once again, our operandi is charged for a full cycle. Personally, I blame your sojourn in Hollywood for these histrionics. Too many actors' hairy buttocks in too many mirrored ceilings.'

She half-whispers, half-growls: 'It *really* isn't in your best interests to speak to me like that, Brother.'

'Oh? Will you take another unannounced sabbatical to the Chilean Andes to divine the meaning of metalife? Go, by all means. Do you good. Inhabit some Indian peasant. Or an alpaca. I'll drive you to the airport after dinner. You'll be back. The operandi's bigger than both of us, baby.'

'The operandi's sixty years old. To cut ourselves off from the Shaded Way—'

'—avoids unwanted attention from the only people alive who could cause us trouble. We're demigods in thrall to no one. Can we *please* keep it that way?'

'We're in thrall to this risible pantomime every nine years,' replies Norah acidly. 'We're in thrall to these' – she indicates her body with disgust – 'birth-bodies to anchor our souls in the world of day. We're in thrall to luck ensuring that nothing goes wrong.'

I'm still not breathing and I feel like my skull's starting to contract. Desperately, fiercely, I think the word *Help!*

'Can we please dine now?' asks Jonah. 'Unless you plan to kill the operandi in a fit of pique?'

My skull throbs painfully as my body groans for air. *Please! I can't breathe*—

Norah exhales like a moody adolescent and grudgingly nods. The Grayer twins' hands then begin to weave through the air like Todd Cosgrove's did earlier, leaving short-lived scratch marks on the dark air. Their lips move and a murmur grows louder as something solidifies above the candle, cell by cell; a kind of fleshy jellyfish, pulsing with reds and purples. It would be pretty if it weren't something from an alien horror movie. Tendrils grow out of it, tendrils with sub-tendrils. Some of them twist through the air towards me, and one pauses for a moment an inch from my eye. I see a tiny orifice at its tip, opening and closing like a carp, before it plunges up my left nostril. Luckily I barely feel it or the others as they worm into my mouth, up my right nostril and into my ears, though I feel a sudden drill-bit of pain in my forehead and see, in the mirror opposite, a shimmering something oozing through one of my mask's eyeholes. It gathers in a small clear sphere in front of my eyes. Tiny luminous plankton hover inside it. So souls are real, it seems.

My soul's the most beautiful thing I've ever seen.

But now the Grayer twins close in on both sides.

No! You can't! It's mine! Please! Nonono—

They purse their lips like they're about to whistle.

Help help help Freya Freya anyone help help I need—

The twins inhale, stretching my soul into an oval.

Someone'llstopyouonedayyou'llsufferyou'llpay—

My soul splits in two. Norah inhales one half, Jonah the other.

Their faces look like Piers's did that night in Malvern . . .

. . . and now it's over. They're sitting back where they were.

The tendril things have gone. The glowing lump has gone.

The Grayers are as still as sculptures. So is the candle flame. In the mirror, a Miss Piggy mask slaps the floor.

YOU
DARK
HORSE
YOU

2006

I nodded off for long enough to slip into a stressful dream. I dreamed I got cold feet about meeting Fred Pink here this evening. Halfway across the cold park I turned back, but a black and orange jogger sprayed a blast into my face from an asthma inhaler. Then I saw a woman in a wheel-chair being pushed by Tom Cruise. Her face was hidden by a raincoat hood and Tom Cruise said, 'Go right ahead, take a look.' So I lifted the hood and saw she was me. Then we were travelling down a narrow alley and someone said, 'You pay an army for a thousand days to use it on one.' Last of all was a black slab like the black slabs in *2001: A Space Odyssey* and as it opened I heard Sally saying, 'You have to wake *up*,' so I did and here I am, alone, in the upstairs room at The Fox and Hounds. As arranged. It's seedier than how I remember it from 1997. The tables are scarred, the chairs are rickety, the wallpaper's scraggy and the carpet's the colour of dried vomit. My tomato juice sits in a smeary glass. Liquified roadkill. The Fox and Hounds is on its last legs, clearly. Downstairs there are only six drinkers at the bar and one of them is a dog for the blind – and on a Saturday evening. The sole nod to alcofrolic jollity is an old-time enamelled Guinness ad, screwed to the wall over the blocked-up fireplace, with a leprechaun playing a fiddle for a dancing toucan. I wonder if that leprechaun noticed Sally nine years ago, and if she noticed him. They sat up here, the 'X-Files Six'. Several witnesses saw my sister and her friends, but nobody agreed at which table they had been sitting.

I press my forehead against the dirty windowpane. In the street below Fred Pink's still having his 'quick catch-up with Misters Benson and Hedges'. The streetlights are coming on. The sun sinks into tarmac-grey clouds, over one-way mazes of brick houses, gasworks, muddy canals, old factories, unloved blocks of flats from the sixties, multi-storey car parks from the seventies, tatty-looking housing from the eighties, a neon-edged multiplex from the nineties. Cul-de-sacs, ring-roads, bus lanes, flyovers. I wish Sally's last known place of abode could have been prettier. For the millionth time I wonder if she's still alive, locked in a madman's attic, praying that we'll never give up, never stop looking. Always I wonder. Sometimes I envy the weeping parents of the definitely dead you see on TV. Grief is an amputation, but hope is incurable haemophilia: you bleed and bleed and bleed. Like Schrödinger's cat inside a box you can never ever open. For the millionth time, I flinch about wriggling out of inviting my sister to New York the summer before she started uni here. Sally wanted to visit, I knew, but I had a job at a photo agency, fashionista friends, invitations to private views, and I was just starting to date women. It was an odd time. Discovering my Real Me *and* babysitting my tubby, dorky, nervy sister had just felt all too much. So I told Sal some bullshit about finding my feet, she pretended to believe me, and I'll never forgive myself. Avril says that not even God can change the past. She's right, but it doesn't help. I get out my mobile and text Avril:

At pub. Real dive. FP no nutter so far but we'll see.
Interview begins in a mo. Home when I can. Xxx

SEND. Avril will be heating up yesterday's lasagna, opening a bottle of wine, settling down to an episode or three of *The Wire*. Wish I was with her. I've known livelier morgues than The Fox and Hounds. The whiskery landlady downstairs tried to crack a funny when we came in: 'Evening, dearie, you must be Our Fred's latest girlfriend, then. Fred, you dark horse you – what magazine you order this one out of, eh?' I should've said, '*Hot Ukrainian Dykes Weekly*.' When the landlady learned I'm a journalist with an interest in Slade Alley, she turned frosty and her 'dearie' grew thorns: 'That's the media for you, innit? Why let a sleeping dog lie when you can flog a dead horse, eh, dearie? Eh?'

Footsteps clomp up the stairs. I get out my Sony digital recorder, a gift from Dad and Sook, aka Mrs John Timms III, and put it on the table. In walks Fred Pink, a withered grey man in a tatty brown coat and a schoolboy's leather satchel that must be half a century old. 'Sorry to keep you, Miss Timms. I do need my little fix.' He's got a gruff, friendly voice you want to trust.

'No problem,' I say. 'Will this table do?'

'Best seat in the house.' He puts his beer on the table, sits down like the old man he is and rubs his skin-and-bone hands. His face is pocked, saggy and spiky with bristles. His glasses are fixed with duct tape. 'Bloomin' parky out. This smoking ban'll be the death of us, I tell you; if cancer don't get us, the double pneumonia will. Still can't get my head round not smoking – in a pub? Political correctness gone mad, that's what it is. Ever interview Tony Blair or Gordon Brown or that lot, do you, in your line of work?'

'Only in press packs. You have to be at the top of the food chain for a private audience. Mr Pink, could I record our interview? That way I can concentrate on what you're saying without taking notes.'

'Record away.' He doesn't add, 'and call me Fred', so I won't. I press RECORD and speak into the microphone: 'Interview with Fred Pink at The Fox and Hounds pub, Saturday twenty-eighth October, 2006, 7.20 p.m.' I swivel the recorder so the mike's facing him. 'Ready when you are.'

The old man takes a deep breath. 'Well. First thing to say is, once you've been a psychiatric patient, no one ever gives you the benefit of the doubt again. Easier to fix a bad credit rating than a bad credibility rating.' Fred Pink speaks with care, as if he's writing his words in permanent ink. 'But whether you believe me or not, Miss Timms,

I'm guilty. Guilty. See, I'm the one who told my nephew Alan about Slade Alley, about Gordon Edmonds, about Nathan and Rita Bishop, about the nine-year cycle. It was me who whetted Alan's appetite. Alan'd told me there was twenty or thirty of them in his club so I reckoned, safety in numbers. Atemporals fear exposure, see. Six kids vanishing was big news, for sure, but twenty or thirty? They'd never dare. All sorts'd've come running: MI7, FBI if any Americans were involved, my friend David Icke; the whole bloomin' shebangle'd be all over Slade House like a dose of the clap. If I'd known Alan's group was down to six, I'd've told him, 'Too risky, just forget it.' And if I'd done that, my nephew, and your sister, and Lance Matthews, Todd Cosgrove, Angelica Gibbons and Fern Penhaligon, they'd still be here, living their lives, with jobs, boyfriends, girlfriends, mortgages. Knowing that's a torment, Miss Timms. A never-ending torment.' Fred Pink swallows, clenches his jaw and shuts his eyes. I write 'Atemporal?' and 'David Icke' in my notebook to give him time to compose himself. 'Sorry, Miss Timms, I . . .'

'I've got regrets about Sally too,' I assure him. 'But I think you're being too hard on yourself.'

Fred Pink dabs his eyes with an old tissue and sips his bitter. He stares at the Guinness-drinking leprechaun.

'In your email you mentioned a backstory, Mr Pink,' I prompt.

'I did. The backstory's why I asked to meet you here this evening. If we did this on the phone, you'd hang up.

Even face to face, in places, you'll think, "Ruddy Nora, the mad old wreck's lost the plot." But hear me out. It leads to Sally.'

'I'm a journalist. I know reality's complex.' I remember Avril using those very words – a 'mad old wreck' – when she read Fred Pink's first email a couple of weeks ago. But I tell the old man, 'I'm listening.'

'We'll kick off over a century ago then, near Ely in Norfolk, at a stately home called Swaffham Manor. Nowadays a Saudi Arabian pal of Prince Charles owns the place, but back then it was the ancestral seat of a family called the Chetwynd-Pitts, who you'll find in the *Domesday Book*, if you please. In 1899, twins was born at Swaffham, a girl and a boy. Not in the big house, mind, but in the gamekeeper's cottage on the edge of the estate. The father was Gabriel Grayer, the mother was his wife, Nellie Grayer, and the twins was named Norah and Jonah. They never got to know their father that well, 'cause Gabriel Grayer got shot three years later by a toff who mistook his peasants for his pheasants, so to speak. Lord and Lady Chetwynd-Pitt felt guilty about the accident, so they let Nellie Grayer and the children stay on in the gamekeeper's cottage. More than that, they took care of Norah and Jonah's schooling, and when Nellie Grayer died of rheumatic fever in 1910, the twin orphans moved into Swaffham Manor proper.'

'You've done a lot of research,' I tell Fred Pink.

'It's my hobby, like. Well, my life, really. You should see

my flat. It's all papers and files, everywhere. Now: you'll have heard stories about the empathy between twins, I'm guessing. Y'know, where one twin gets hit by a bus in Istanbul, say, and the other falls over in London at the exact same moment. But did you know that twins'll sometimes speak a language that only they understand, specially when they're still learning to talk?'

'As a matter of fact, yes. When I lived in Manhattan I used to babysit for toddler triplets who talked in their own private dialect. It was amazing to hear.'

'Well, events took place at Swaffham Manor what suggested Norah and Jonah Grayer combined these two skills. To call a spade a spade: telepathy.' Fred Pink gives me a probing look. 'Do we have a problem with telepathy, Miss Timms?'

My nutter-detector glows amber. 'I am rather a fan of proof, Mr Pink.'

'So am I. So am I. Albertina Chetwynd-Pitt – Her Ladyship – published a memoir in 1925 called *Rivers Old And Lost*. It's all about what I'm telling you now: the twins, their upbringing, and everything. In it, she says how one January evening in 1910, she, her daughters and Norah Grayer were all playing cribbage in the drawing room at Swaffham. All of a sudden, Norah cried out, dropped her cards, and said that Arthur, the eldest Chetwynd-Pitt boy, had fallen off his horse at Poole's Brook – over a mile away from the manor – and couldn't move. He needed a stretcher and the doctor, right away. Lady Albertina was

147

shocked that Norah'd tell such a baseless fib. But Norah begged her to send help, 'cause, and I quote, "Jonah is with him and Jonah is telling me." By now the Chetwynd-Pitt daughters were properly spooked too, so against her better judgement, Lady Albertina sent a servant running off – who found the scene as Norah'd described it, in every detail.'

I reach for my tomato juice but it still looks like roadkill and I change my mind. 'It's a tasty anecdote, but how is it "proof"?'

Fred Pink takes out his Benson & Hedges, remembers the smoking ban and puts the cigarettes back, tetchily. 'The day after, the twins were interviewed by Lord and Lady Chetwynd-Pitt with their friend Dean Grimond of Ely Cathedral. Dean Grimond was a no-nonsense hard-boiled Scot who'd been an army chaplain in the Crimea and had none of the airy-fairy about him. He ordered the twins to tell him how Norah'd known about Arthur coming off his horse at Poole's Brook. So the twins confessed they'd been able to "telegram" thoughts for years, but kept it a secret 'cause they'd noticed it scared people and drew attention to them. Like you, Miss Timms, Lord Chetwynd-Pitt wanted proof, so he devised this experiment. He gave Norah a pencil and paper, led Jonah to the billiards room in Swaffham Manor, and read out a random line from *The Jungle Book*. His Lordship then asked Jonah to "telegram" the line to Norah, back in the library. Jonah shut his eyes for a few seconds, then said the job was done. They both went back to the library to find that Norah had written down the very same line from Kipling.' Fred Pink looks at me as if the matter is now beyond dispute.

I say, 'Remarkable,' but think, *If all this actually took place.*

'Next, Dean Grimond got Norah to "telegram" a verse from St John's Gospel.' Fred Pink shuts his eyes: '"He that followeth me shall not walk in darkness, but shall have the light of life." Back in the billiards room Jonah wrote it down, word-perfect. Lastly, Lady Albertina wanted a turn. She had Jonah "telegram" a verse from a nursery rhyme in German. Norah wrote it word-perfect, though with a few spelling mistakes. Neither of the twins knew a word of German, see.' Fred Pink slurps his bitter and dabs his cracked lips with the frayed sleeve of his jacket. 'The upshot? Dean Grimond told the twins that some of God's gifts are better left unexamined, and that they shouldn't refer to their "telegrams" in public, "lest excitable persons be tempted down wrong paths". Norah and Jonah promised to obey. Dean Grimond gave them both a humbug and went back to his cathedral. Nice work if you can get it.'

A TV roar of disappointment wafts up the stairs. Checking my Sony's still working, I ask, 'How do you know Lady Albertina is a trustworthy source?'

Fred Pink rubs his scalp and dandruff falls. 'Same way you judge your sources, I imagine, Miss Timms. By developing a nose for a lie, an ear for a fib, and an eye for a tell. Right? Lady Chetwynd-Pitt's book is detailed where a fraud would gloss over stuff, and rough where a liar would polish it better. Anyway, where's her motive for lying? Not money – she was loaded. Not attention – she only had a hundred copies of her book printed, and by the time it was published she was a virtual recluse, like.'

I swivel my gold ring from Avril round my finger. 'In journalism, we try to cross-corroborate an informant's more contentious claims.'

'"Cross-corroborate". Good word. I'll store that away. It's time you met Dr Léon Cantillon.' Fred Pink unfastens his satchel, takes out a dog-eared folder and produces a laser-scanned copy of an old hand-tinted photograph of a man of about forty. He's wearing a French Foreign Legion uniform, a raffish smile, a couple of medals and, round his neck, a stethoscope. The caption underneath reads *Le docteur L. Cantillon, Légion étrangère, Ordre national de la Légion d'honneur, Croix de guerre.* 'Léon Cantillon. Colourful figure, you might say. Born in 1874 in Dublin in an old French Huguenot family; grew up speaking French; studied medicine at Trinity College, but he had a hot-headed streak and had to leave Ireland after shooting the son of a member of Parliament in a duel, no less. Bang. Straight between the eyes, dead before he hit the deck. Cantillon joined the French Foreign Legion a few months later – we're up to 1895 now – and served as a medic in the Mandingo War on the Ivory Coast, and later in the South-Oranese Campaign. Dirty little wars in the carve-up of Africa, these – even the French've forgotten 'em nowadays. Cantillon had a knack for languages, too. When he wasn't doctoring and soldiering he was learning Arabic, and claims he spoke it fluently by 1905, when he got himself a plum job at the Legion's hospital in Algiers. It was in Algiers that his interest in the occult took root, by his own account. He mingled with Prussian the-osophists, Armenian spiritualists, Ibadi Muslim shamans, Hasidic Kabbalists, and one mystic in particular who lived south of Algiers in the foothills of the Atlas Mountains. He's known as the Albino Sayyid of Aït Arif, and by and by he'd be playing a major role in the Grayers' lives.'

This is all sounding a bit *Da Vinci Code* for me. 'What's your source for all of this, Mr Pink? Lady Albertina's book?'

'No. Léon Cantillon wrote his memoir too, see. *The Great Unveiling.* My own copy's one of just ten known survivors, and it's this account what cross-corroborates Lady Albertina's story, so to speak.' He turns away to cough a smoker's cough into the crook of his elbow. It lasts a good while. 'So. Dr Cantillon met Lord Chetwynd-Pitt in early summer of 1915 at the house of mutual friends in London. After a few schooners of port, His Lordship began telling the soldier–doctor about Lady Albertina's "chronic hysteria". The poor woman was in a terrible state by this point. In March of 1915, all three of Lord and Lady Chetwynd-Pitt's sons'd been gassed, blown up or machine-gunned *in the very same week* at the Battle of Neuve Chapelle. All three. Imagine that: on Monday, you've got three sons, by Friday you've got none. Lady Albertina had just, y'know, caved in. Physically, mentally, spiritually, brutally. Her husband hoped that Léon Cantillon, as a sympathetic spiritualist and a man of medicine, might be the man to help where everyone else'd failed, like. To bring her back from the brink.'

Fred Pink's framed by the window. Dusk's falling. 'So the Chetwynd-Pitts had been dabbling in spiritualism since the "telegram incident", had they?'

'They had, Miss Timms, they had. The craze for séances was in full swing, see, and the likes of Sir Arthur Conan Doyle no less was saying it was founded in science. To be sure, there was no shortage of shysters all too happy to milk the craze, but thanks to Norah and Jonah, the Chetwynd-Pitts knew that *some* psychic phenomena, at least, was genuine. As a matter of fact, Lord Chetwynd-Pitt'd brought several mediums up to Ely to channel the spirits of their dead boys, but none of them'd proved themselves to be the real McCoy, and with each dashed hope Lady Albertina's sanity took a fresh battering.'

I bring the tomato juice to my lips, but it still looks like a specimen jar in a blood bank. 'And could Dr Cantillon help?'

Fred Pink rubs his wiry bristles. 'Well, after a fashion, yes – though he never claimed to be a medium. After examining Lady Albertina, Cantillon said that her grief'd "severed her ethereal cord to her spirit guide". He performed a healing ritual he'd learned off of a shaman in the mountains of Rif and prescribed an "elixir". In her book, Lady Albertina wrote that the elixir gave her a vision of "an angel rolling away a stone from her entombment" and she saw her three sons happy on a higher plane. In *his* book, Cantillon mentions that his elixir contained a new wonder drug called cocaine, so make of that what you will. I'd add to the mix the benefits of the talking cure as well. The chance for an Edwardian lady to spill her guts in private and vent her spleen at God, king and country must've been therapeutic, to say the least. Like grief counselling, nowadays. Certainly at this stage in the proceedings, Dr Cantillon seems to've been a very welcome guest indeed.'

My phone buzzes in my bag. Avril texting me back, I expect, but I ignore it. 'Where are the Grayer twins in all this?'

'Right: Jonah was an apprentice clerk in the Swaffham Manor estate office. Short-sightedness and a dicky ticker'd saved him from the trenches, though as these conditions never troubled him in later life, I can't help but wonder how real they were. Norah was a weekly boarder at a school for ladies in Cambridge, to up her marriage pro-spects. Léon Cantillon'd heard about their "telegrams" from the Chetwynd-Pitts, of course, so the first chance he had, he asked for a demo. It took place on the doctor's first weekend at Swaffham. He was impressed. He was *very* impressed. "An annunciation of the New Age of Man", he later called it. A fortnight later, Cantillon put a proposal to his hosts. If they "lent" him Norah and Jonah, and if the twins was willing, he'd "provide a psychic education consummate with their gifts." The doctor said he knew an occultic teacher who'd train the twins in spirit channelling. Once Norah and Jonah'd mastered that skill, he said, Lady Albertina'd be able to freely speak with her sons from their higher plane, without fear of being gulled by swindlers.'

I sniff a swindler. 'How for real was Dr Cantillon?'

The old man rubs a watery blue, red-rimmed eye and growls thoughtfully. 'Well, the Chetwynd-Pitts believed him, which is what matters to our backstory. They agreed to his proposal to educate Norah and Jonah, but here's where the doctor's version of events and Lady Albertina's begin to part ways. She wrote that Léon Cantillon'd promised the twins'd be away no more than a few months. Cantillon's claim is that the Chetwynd-Pitts gave him guardianship of the Grayers with no small print about expiry dates, time or distance. Who's telling the truth? That I can't tell you. Truth has this habit of changing after the fact, don't you find? What we do know is that Léon Cantillon took the twins first to Dover, crossed over to Calais, passed through wartime Paris, carried on south to Marseille, then sailed by steamship to Algiers. Lady Albertina calls this journey "an abduction, no more, no less", but by the time she and her husband found out about it, the horse'd bolted. Repatriation of minors is tricky enough now. Back then, when sixteen-year-olds were adults in most senses, and with the Great War in top gear, so to speak, and inside French colonial jurisprudence – forget it. The Grayer twins were gone.'

I'm not clear: 'Were they taken against their will?'

Fred Pink's face says *Hardly likely*. 'Which would you choose? Life as an orphaned pleb in the Tory Fens in wartime England, or life as a student of the occult under the Algerian stars?'

'It would depend on whether I believed in the occult.'

'They believed.' Fred Pink sips his bitter. 'Sally did too.'

And if she hadn't, I think, *she wouldn't have been playing Ghostbusters in unfamiliar backstreets at night; and whatever happened to her wouldn't have happened*. Either I bite my tongue or I kill the interview. 'The Grayers stayed in Algeria, then.'

'They did, yes. Norah and Jonah already knew telepathy. What other powers might they acquire, in the right hands? Léon Cantillon was a sly operator, there's no doubt, but a sly operator can still be the right man for the job.' He looks at Léon Cantillon's photo again. 'He took the twins to the Albino Sayyid of Aït Arif. I mentioned him before. The Sayyid followed an occult branch called la Voie Ombragée, or the Shaded Way, and lived in a "dwelling of many rooms" by a fast-flowing stream at a "high neck of a secret valley" a day's ride from Algiers; and that's about all the info Cantillon gives us. The Sayyid accepted the odd foreign twins – who couldn't speak a word of Arabic at this point, remember – as disciples in his house, so he must've seen potential in them. Cantillon returned to his duties at the Foreign Legion hospital in Algiers, though he made the journey to the Sayyid's once a fortnight to check up on his young charges' progress.'

Outside the pub, a woman hollers, 'You're s'posed to indicate, moron!' and a car roars off. 'Mr Pink,' I say. 'If I can be frank, this story feels a long way away from my sister's disappearance.'

Fred Pink nods, and frowns at the clock on the wall: 8.14. 'Give me till nine o'clock. If I haven't connected all of this with your Sally and my Alan by then, I'll call you a taxi. On my honour.'

While I don't have Fred Pink marked down as a liar, I do have him marked down as a dreamer-upper of alternative histories. On the other hand, after all these years my own enquiries into Sally's disappearance have led exactly nowhere. Maybe Fred Pink's tracking me down is a hint that I need to look for leads in less obvious places. Starting now. 'Okay: nine o'clock. Was channelling dead spirits on the Sayyid's syllabus, as Cantillon had promised Lady Albertina?'

'You've got a knack of asking the right question, Miss Timms.' Fred Pink gets out a box of spearmint Tic Tacs, shakes out three, offers me one – I refuse – and puts all three in his mouth. 'No. Léon Cantillon had lied to the Chetwynd-Pitts about séances. I think he knew perfectly well that séances are almost always fraud. When you die, your soul crosses the Dusk between life and the Blank

Sea. The journey takes forty-nine days, but there's no Wi-Fi there, so to speak, so no messages can be sent. Either way. Mediums might convince themselves they're hearing voices from the dead, but the boring reality is, it's impossible.'

Well, that's wacko. 'That's very exact. Forty-nine days?'

Fred Pink shrugs. 'The speed of sound's very exact. So's pi. So are chemical formulas.' He crunches his Tic Tacs. 'Ever been to the Atlas Mountains in North Africa, Miss Timms?' I shake my head. 'I have, believe it or not, just a few years back. Thanks to three thousand quid I won on a scratch-card. Goes a bloomin' long way in Algeria, does three thousand pounds, if you watch out for the pickpockets and rip-off merchants. Those buckled-up mountains, the dry sky, the hot wind, the . . . oh, the whole massive . . . otherness of it, so to speak. I'll never forget it. Rewires your head, if you stay there too long. Little wonder all the hippies and that lot made a beeline for places like Marrakesh in the sixties. Places change you, Miss Timms, and deserts change us pale Northerners so much, our own mothers wouldn't recognise us. Day by day, the twins' Englishness ebbed away. They picked up Arabic from the Sayyid's other disciples; they ate flatbread, hummus and figs; Jonah let his beard grow; Norah wore a veil, like a good Muslim girl; and sandals and dishdashas made more sense in that climate than shoes and cufflinks and petticoats and what have you. The calendar lost its meaning for the twins, Cantillon writes. One, two, three years passed. They learned occult arts and obscure sciences that there aren't even words for in English, things that not one mind in a hundred thousand learns, or *could* learn, even if the chance came along. The Grayers' only link with the outside world was Dr Cantillon, but when he brought them up to speed with that world – the slaughter in Flanders, the fallout from Gallipoli, the killings in Mesopotamia; the politics in Westminster, in Berlin, in Paris, in Washington – to Norah and Jonah it all sounded like stuff going on in places they'd read about years ago. Not real. For the twins, home was their Sayyid's valley. Their fatherland and motherland was the Shaded Way.' Fred Pink scratches his itchy neck – he appears to suffer from mild psoriasis – and stares through my head, all the way to a moonlit dwelling in the Atlas Mountains.

The cracked clock says 8.18. 'How long were they there?'

'Until April 1919. It ended as suddenly as it'd begun, like. Cantillon visited the Sayyid one day and the master told him he'd taught the twins all the knowledge he could impart. The time'd come for the great globe itself to be their master, he said. Which meant what, exactly? And where? England held no great attraction for any of them. There'd be no fond welcome home from the Chetwynd-Pitts at Swaffham Manor, that was for sure. Ireland was having birth pangs and gearing up for a vicious civil war. France was on its knees, along with most of Europe, Algiers's boom years as a war port were over, and Léon

Cantillon, who was always better at spending money than earning it, now found himself with a pair of oddball semi-Arabised English twins in tow. How to convert the Grayers' occultic knowledge into a well-padded lifestyle, that was the doctor's dilemma, wasn't it? And the answer? The good old US of A, that was the answer. The three of them sailed for New York in July, second class, with Cantillon posing as the twins' Uncle Léon. Norah and Jonah were hungry to see the world, like gap-year kids nowadays. They took a town-house on Klinker Street in Greenwich Village.'

'I know it well,' I say. '*Spyglass*'s New York office is on Klinker Street.'

'Is that a fact?' Fred Pink sips his bitter and suppresses a belch. ''Scuse me. Small world.'

'What did they do to earn a living in the States?'

Fred Pink gives me a knowing look. 'They held séances.'

'But séances are fraudulent, you just said.'

'I did. They are. And I'm not here to defend Cantillon or the twins, Miss Timms, but they weren't hucksters in the usual manner. See, Norah and Jonah could read minds, or "overhear" the thoughts of most people they came across. *That* bit wasn't a trick. It was just an extra sense they had, like extremely sensitive hearing. They could rummage through their clients' minds and discover things no-one knew, not even the people whose minds they were in. The twins knew what their grief-stricken clients most needed to hear, and what words'd best heal them – and those were the words they said. The only fiction was the claim that these words came from the dear departed. Now you might say that's worse, not better, and maybe you'd be right. But is it so far away from what your shrinks and counsellors and psychowhatnots try to do nowadays? There was a lot, and I do mean a *lot*, of unhappy and despairing and downright suicidal New Yorkers who left that little house on Klinker Street certain, quite certain, that their loved ones were in a better place and looking out for them and that one day they'd be reunited. I mean, that's what religion does, doesn't it? Are you going to condemn every priest and imam and rabbi on earth for doing the very same thing? No, the Grayer twins' séances weren't real; but yes, the hope they gave was. Isn't the yes better than the no?'

Fraud's fraud, I think, but I perform an ambiguous nod. 'So the New York gigs went well.'

'Very. Cantillon was a canny manager. Once the Grayers got a bit of a name for themselves, he switched tack: discreet appointments at wealthy clients' homes. No props, no smoke, no mirrors, no ectoplasm, no Ouija, no daft voices. No public performances, nothing vulgar or theatrical. Just quiet, calm, sane grief-relief, so to speak. "Your son says this" and "Your sister says that". If Cantillon felt a possible client was only a thrill seeker, he turned them down. Or so he claimed, anyway.'

A football chant from the TV below wafts upstairs. It's a choppy, lulling and otherworldly sound. 'If the Grayers had an array of genuine psychic powers, why content themselves with telling consoling fibs to rich Americans?'

Fred Pink shrugs like a comedy Frenchman: palms raised, shoulders high and head low. 'Cantillon's motives I'll guess at – money – but Norah and Jonah left no written account, so who's to say? Maybe they saw themselves as students of humanity and séances let them study people better. They had a serious case of wanderlust, too, and their séance service, let's call it, was a passport valid in all territories. Personal recommendations smoothed their way, and Uncle Léon and his niece and nephew never travelled second-class again. In the spring of 1920 they moved to Boston, in autumn it was Charleston, then New Orleans, then San Francisco. Why stop there? They took a liner to Hawaii, then to Yokohama. After a spell in Japan, they travelled on to Peking, Manchuria, Shanghai, Hong Kong, Macau, Ceylon. The best hotels and the houses of the grateful rich were their homes in that period. Bombay, New Delhi. A year or two in the British Raj, why not? A summer up in the hill stations. Then Aden, Suez, Cairo, Cyprus, Constantinople, Athens. A winter in Rome, a spring in Vienna, a summer in Berlin, Christmas in Paris. In his book, Cantillon describes how the twins honed their arts as they travelled, seeing the sights, and "settled for a brief sojourn like exotic birds in whatever Society they found themselves in" – Norah rejected no less than six proposals of marriage and no doubt Jonah enjoyed his share of liaisons and conquests – but always they carried on west-wards till one drizzly day in May 1925 the Dover train trundled into Victoria Station, and the Grayers and their guardian took a cab to a house in Queen's Gardens, a swish and leafy street in Bayswater.'

'They financed five years of luxury globetrotting with séances?'

'They diversified a bit once they left the States. Disciples of the Shaded Way learn the art of suasion. A tackier name is "mind control". Maybe you can guess, Miss Timms, how a talent like that might be turned into a few bob . . .'

I play along: 'If "suasioning" were real, you could enlist a nearby millionaire to make you out a humongous bank draft.'

Fred Pink's face suggests I guessed correctly. 'And after, you use another Shaded Way skill – redaction – to erase your generous benefactor's memory of ever writing the cheque. Some'd call it the perfect crime; others'd call it survival; a socialist'd call it the redistribution of wealth.' Fred Pink stands up. 'Might I just pop to the gents, Miss Timms? The beer was a mistake; my prostate's not what it was . . .'

I indicate the doorway. 'I'm not going anywhere.' *Yet.*

'Aren't you drinking your tomato juice, Miss Timms?'

I look at it. 'I, uh, just don't really fancy it, after all.'

'I'll bring you something else up. Listening's thirsty work.'

I wave him away. 'No need, really.'

Fred Pink makes a mock-glum face. 'Ah, but I insist.'

'A bit later.'

When he's gone, I turn off my digital recorder. It's all

saved – not that I'll ever listen to it again. Only an all-out conspiracy theorist or the mentally ill would connect this Norfolk-Dublin-Algeria-America-Trans-Pacific-Mysterious-Orient tale with six students who went missing in 1997. It's tempting just to slip away now, while there are still lots of trains back to London. Really, what could Fred Pink do if I did a runner now? Send me a pissed-off email? I'm a journalist: I get twenty pissed-off emails per hour. Fred Pink's spent nine years of his life in a coma, more years locked away in a secure ward beyond Slough's outer reaches, and he's an obvious believer in the dark arts. The man's brain is scrambled. But no. I gave him my word to stay until nine o'clock, so I'll stay. It's now 8.27. The last text was from Avril, as I thought.

O de glamour! Bt seriously hope Mr P isnt waste of time. Text me if u need urgent emrgncy 2 escape 2.

I reply:

Jury still out re Mr P but will probly get train about 930 back to Padders 10 home by 11 i hope xxx

SEND. I don't remember eating dinner so I suppose I must have missed it. I go downstairs to the bar to see if there's anything to eat. The place looks like a stage set, and rather a cash-strapped one at that. With the departure of the blind chap and his dog, the population of The Fox and Hounds has dwindled to four. Up on the plasma screen a red team are playing a blue team, but I don't know who is who. Avril knows that MUN means Manchester United and ARS stands for Arsenal, but I can never work the names out. It's a corner, and the landlady waits a few seconds to watch the outcome – no goal – before dragging herself over to my end of the bar. I ask if she sells snacks and she lets a long pause elapse to illustrate her contempt for metropolitan media dykes. 'Cheese and onion crisps or ready salted; dry roasted peanuts, or honey-glazed cashews. That's it.'

Wow, an embarrassment of riches. 'Two bags of cashews and a diet tonic water, with lemon. Please.'

'We only sell real tonic water. Not diet.'

'Looks like I'll have a real tonic water, then. Thank you so much.'

The landlady plucks the nuts from a rack, takes the tonic water from a shelf below, flips off the cap, retrieves a glass, drops in a limp segment of lemon, and pecks at the till with her bony index finger. 'Three pounds forty-five.' I hand over the right money. She asks, 'What paper d'you write for, then?'

'*Spyglass*. It's a magazine.'

'Never heard of it.'

'It's bigger in the States than it is here.'

'Like *Private Eye*, is it? One o'those sarcastic papers?'

'No, not really,' I say. 'It's less satirical.'

'So why do Americans give two hoots about six students

who disappeared in a small English city nine years ago?'

'I'm not sure if they do. My editor will decide that. But I'm curious.' I consider telling the landlady about Sally, but I don't. 'Being curious is my job.'

'It's ancient history, all that stuff is.' She glances at the gents, and leans close enough for me to see the evidence of an exhausting life beneath her coating of make-up. 'You're not doing Fred any favours by egging him on. He blames himself for Alan's vanishing, which really is mental. He spent six years at Dawkins Hospital, locked up with the Teletubbies – you *do* know that, yeah?'

'Mr Pink's been open about his medical history, yes.'

The landlady's jaw chews phantom gum. 'Meanwhile he fancies himself as this Inspector Morse who'll solve the big mystery and maybe find Alan and the X-Files Six alive somewhere, which is double-mental. "X-Files Six": as if it's all some stupid TV show! But it's not. It's serious. It's pain. It's best left buried. Fred's wife left him, in the end. A saint of a woman was Jackie, but when Fred buggered off to Algeria even she couldn't take it any more and moved back to the Isle of Man. Now all Fred ever thinks about are his theories about his Illuminati, the Holy Grail, Atlantis and whateverthebollocks it is this week. And you,' she folds her meaty arms as Fred Pink emerges from the gents in the corner, '*you*, you're feeding all that. Pouring fuel on the flames. Hey, Fred.' She straightens up and smiles at Fred Pink like nothing's wrong. 'Your new best friend here was telling me how low *some* media scum-suckers'll stoop just to get a story. Throw 'em to the bloody piranhas, I say. Let like eat like. Fancy a brandy this time, eh?'

'Sorry about Maggs,' says Fred Pink, back in the upstairs room. 'I shouldn't've told her you're a journalist. The locals'd rather forget the X-Files Six. Too Amityville Horror, too Bermuda Triangle. Bad for house prices.'

I munch a handful of honey-glazed cashews. God, they're good. '"Scum-sucker" is one of the sweeter names I've been called, believe me. So, Mr Pink: we left Dr Cantillon and the Grayer twins in Bayswater after their years of travel in foreign parts.'

Fred Pink sloshes his brandy around the glass. 'Yes, it's now 1925. Norah and Jonah are twenty-six, and Uncle Léon is fifty. For ten years he's been their fixer, guardian, PR man, accountant. Now he wants to be their biographer, or more – their John the Baptist. You see, he'd decided the time'd come to go public and persuade the world that spiritualism and science could be respectably married. Money and a comfortable life wasn't enough, you see. His new ambition was to establish a new discipline – psycho-soterica – with none other than Dr Léon Cantillon as its Darwin, its Freud, its Newton. Which put him at serious odds with Norah and Jonah. See, they'd drunk their fill of the big bad world by this stage. What they wanted was to hide away and see which dead ends down the Shaded Way might not be dead ends after all. So they told Cantillon no, there'd be no biography, no great unveiling, and no more public engagements. Obedient Uncle Léon told the twins, "I hear and obey." But Obedient Uncle Léon was lying through his teeth. He spent most of the next two years writing his big masterpiece, *The Great Unveiling*. It wasn't the usual rehash of Europe's Top Ten Witches and Wizards, like most books about the occult were in those days. Leon Cantillon's book had three sections. Part One was the first ever written history of the Shaded Way, from its fifth-century beginnings to the twentieth. Part Two was a biography of the Grayer twins from their Swaffham Manor days to their return to England. Part Three was a manifesto for an International Psychosoterica Society to be set up in London, with Dr Guess Who as its lifetime president.'

My phone buzzes in my bag. Avril's reply to my reply, I bet. It's 8.45, it'll wait. 'Why did Cantillon go against the twins' wishes?'

'Can't be sure. I suspect he reckoned that once the cat was out of the bag, once Uncle Tom Cobley and all were clamouring for the Age of Psychosoterica to begin, the Grayers'd see how right he was after all and sign up. If that *was* Cantillon's thinking,' Fred Pink ruffles more dandruff out of his hair, 'he was mistaken. Tragically mistaken. On March twenty-ninth, 1927, the printers delivered ten boxes of *The Great Unveiling*. On March thirtieth, the good doctor mailed about six dozen copies to various theosophists, philosophers, occultists and patrons, in England and overseas.

My copy of the book, which I keep in a safety deposit box in a place I tell nobody, is one of those six dozen. In the early hours of the next morning – March thirty-first – a conveniently positioned bobby was walking down Queen's Gardens. He saw Léon Cantillon lift his fifth-floor sash window and perch on the sill, naked as a baby, and shout out these words: "The mind is its own place, and in itself can make a heaven of hell, a hell of heaven" – John Milton, if you're curious. Then he jumped. He might've survived, but he landed on a row of pointy railings. You can picture the scene. Quite the nine-day wonder it was. The coroner recorded a verdict of death by insanity and the *Westminster Gazette* covered the funeral. Jonah read the eulogy, while Norah, "the very model of demure grief in an ankle-length dress of black crêpe" – yes, I memorised it – sobbed for her guardian. Jonah told the reporter how he prayed that Dr Cantillon's "bizarre delusions" would show how dangerous it can be to meddle in the black arts. Dean Grimond would've been proud. Weeks passed, the tragedy of the ex-Foreign Legion doctor became old news, and, copy by copy, the large stock of unposted *Great Unveiling*s burned in the Grayers' fireplace in Queen's Gardens.'

I'm bothered by a phrase: '"A conveniently positioned bobby"?'

Fred Pink sips his brandy. 'Never cross a qualified suasioner.'

To follow Fred Pink's trail of breadcrumbs you have to blindfold your own sanity. 'Meaning, a suasioner can also make a man jump to his death?'

''Xactly so, Miss Timms.'

'But Cantillon, in your narrative, had been a loyal friend and protector.'

'"Had been," yes; but then he became a threat. A kind of apostate, too: the occult's like any religious order – or any bunch of extremists, come to that. It's all beer and sunshine and "We are your family" as long as you obey orders, but once you get your own ideas or start talking out of school, the knives come out. Whether Cantillon was pushed or whether Cantillon jumped, the Grayers' trail grows faint after the *Westminster Gazette*, and stays faint for four years. They left the Bayswater house in May 1927 – I date their departure from their launderers' accounts – but then it's a big blank. I've found a possible sighting of the twins at Sainte-Agnès in the Maritime Alps in 1928, a reference to mind-reading English twins in Rhodesia in 1929, and a "Miss Norah" with a twin brother in a love letter sent from Fiji in 1930, but nothing's – what's the word? – cross-corroborated.' Fred Pink drums his fingers on his bulging satchel. 'You've already been patient, so I'll hurry us on to your sister's role before the clock strikes nine.'

'I will need to get going then, Mr Pink.'

'In August 1931, according to the local land register, Mr Jonah Grayer and his sister, Miss Norah Grayer, bought Slade House, a property not two hundred yards from this very pub. It'd been an eighteenth-century rectory attached to the parish of Saint Brianna. Once upon a time it was surrounded by woods and fields, though by the time the

Grayers moved in, Slade House was a walled fortress in a sea of brick houses, in a factory town more passed through than stopped at, so to speak. The neighbourhood was full of factory workers, full of big families, full of Irish and itinerants, full of folk coming and going and doing midnight flits. Which suited the Grayers' purposes down to a T.'

'What purposes were these, Mr Pink?'

'They needed laboratory rats, see.'

What I see is the wackometer needle climbing. 'Laboratory rats for . . . what kind of experiments?'

Fred Pink's glasses reflect and bend the grimy strip-light. 'I'll die, one of these mornings. I'm seventy-nine now, I still smoke like a flamin' chimney, my blood pressure's chronic. Maggs the landlady'll die, too; whoever keeps sending you them texts'll die; and you'll die as well, Miss Timms. Death's life's only guarantee, yes? We all know it, yet we're hardwired to dread it. That dread's our survival instinct and it serves us well enough when we're young, but it's a curse when you're older.'

'I'm sure you're right, Mr Pink. And?'

'Norah and Jonah Grayer wanted to not die. Ever.'

Bang on cue, a goal's scored on the TV downstairs and the crowd surges and roars like a kettle boiling. I maintain my professional face. 'Don't we all?'

'Yes. We do. Life everlasting.' Fred Pink takes off his glasses to rub them on his stained shirt. 'It's why religion got invented and it's why religion stays invented. What else matters more than not dying? Power? Gold? Sex? A million quid? A billion? A trillion? Really? They won't buy you an extra minute when your number's up. No, cheating death, cheating ageing, cheating the care home, cheating the mirror and the dug-up corpse's face like *mine* that you'll see in your mirror too, Miss Timms, and sooner than you think: that's a prize worth the hunting, the taking. That's the *only* prize worth hunting. And what we want, we dream of. The stage props change down the ages, but the dream stays the same: philosophers' stones; magic fountains in lost Tibetan valleys; lichens that slow the decay of our cells; tanks of liquid whatever that'll freeze us for a few centuries; computers that'll store our personalities as ones and zeroes for the rest of time. To call a spade a spade: immortality.'

The wackometer needle is stuck on 11. 'I see.'

Fred Pink's smile curves downwards. 'The one little snag being, immortality's all hooey. Right?'

I sip my non-diet tonic water. 'Since you ask, yes.'

He puts his glasses on. 'What if, *very* occasionally, it's real?'

And so, at 8.52, Fred Pink proves himself divorced not only from his wife but from reality itself. 'If anyone discovered How Not To Die, I don't think it'd stay a secret very long.'

Now he acts as if he's the one humouring me. 'Don't you now? Why's that then, Miss Timms?'

I strangle a sigh of exasperation. 'Because the inventors or researchers would want recognition, fame, Nobel Prizes.'

'No. What they'd want is Not To Die. Which *wouldn't* happen by going public. Think about it: about the squalid, shitty reasons that people murder each other in large numbers now. Oil; the drug trade; control over occupied territories and the word 'occupied'. Water. God's true name, His true will, who owns access to Him. The astonishing belief that Iraq can be turned into Sweden by deposing its dictator and smashing the place up a bit. What *wouldn't* these same warlords, oligarchs, elites and electorates do to enforce their claims over a limited supply of Life Everlasting? Miss Timms, they'd kick off World War Three. Our plucky inventors'd be shot by maniacs, be buried in bunkers or die in a nuclear war. If the supply's *not* limited, the prospects're even bleaker. Yes, we'd all stop dying, but we wouldn't stop breeding. Would we? Men are dogs, Miss Timms; *you* know that. Give it twenty, thirty, fifty years, there'd be thirty, forty, a hundred billion human beings eating up our godforsaken world. We'd be drowning in our own shit even as we fought each other for the last Pot Noodle in the last supermarket. See? Either way you lose. If you're smart enough to discover immortality, you're smart enough to ensure your own supply and keep very very *very* shtum indeed. Like the Grayer twins did, in an attic, close to this spot, eighty years ago.' Fred Pink leans back like a man who's proved a point.

His belief is unshakeable and appalling. I choose my words with care. 'How did the Grayers achieve what you're saying they achieved?'

'A quartet of psychosoteric breakthroughs. First off, they perfected the lacuna. Which is what? A lacuna's a small space that's immune to time, so a candle'll never burn down in it, or a body won't age in it. Second, they enhanced the transversion their Sayyid'd taught them – what the New Age jokers call astral projection – so they could venture out from their bodies, as far as they wanted, for as long as they wanted. Third, they mastered long-term suasioning, so their souls could move into a stranger and occupy that body. Meaning, the Grayers were now free to leave their bodies in the lacuna they created in the attic of Slade House and inhabit bodies in the outside world. You with me so far, yes?'

Yes, Fred Pink is barking mad. 'Assuming souls are real.'

'Souls are as real as gall bladders, Miss Timms. Believe me.'

'And nobody's ever held a soul or X-rayed one because . . . ?'

'Is a mind X-rayable? Is hunger? Is jealousy? Time?'

'I see. So souls can fly about the place, like Tinker Bell?'

A pipe gurgles in the wall. 'Provided the soul in question is the soul of an Engifted.'

'A what?'

'An Engifted. A psychic, or a potential psychic. And like Tinker Bell, sort of; but a Tinker Bell who'll live inside your mind without your consent, for years if it wants, hack into your brain, control your actions and play funny buggers with your memories. Or kill you.'

My phone's vibrating again. 'So the Grayer twins are a pair of wandering Jews hitching rides in hosts while their own bodies stay dry-frozen in a bubble back in Slade House where it's forever 1931?'

Fred Pink knocks back his brandy. '1934. It took them a few years — and a few lab rats — to perfect their modus operandi, so to speak. But there's a catch. This system won't run off the mains. It runs off psychovoltage. The psychovoltage of Engifteds. Every nine years the Grayers have to feed it. They have to lure the right sort of guest into a . . . kind of reality bubble they call an orison. The orison's their fourth breakthrough, by the way. Once the guest's there, the twins have to get them to eat or drink banjax. Banjax is a chemical that shrivels the cord fastening the soul to the body, so it can be extracted just before death.'

What do you say to a delusional old man who expects you to be awed by the historic awesomeness of his revelations? 'That all sounds very involved.'

'Ah, the Grayers make it look easy. It's an art form, see.'

It's batshit crazy is what it is. 8.56. 'And how is it connected with my sister?'

'She was engifted, Miss Timms. The Grayers killed her for her psychovoltage.'

Right. Now I feel like he's just punched me. And I want to punch him back for dragooning my sister into his nutso fantasy.

'I knew it wasn't Alan, and I've met siblings of the other four, but not one had the glow. You do, which finally confirms it was Sally they were after.'

I feel various emotions all too mixed up to sort out, like ingredients flying around in a Moulinex. 'You never even met Sally, Mr Pink.'

'Ah, but her case study leaves little room for doubt. When I read what her doctor in Singapore wrote, I guessed her psychic potential—'

'Excuse me. Stop. When you read *what*?'

'She had therapy in Singapore. You must've known.'

'Of course I knew, but you – you *read* Sally's psychiatric reports?'

'Yes.' Fred Pink looks surprised that I'm upset. 'I had to read them.'

'What gives you the right to read Sal's files? And how did you get them?'

He looks at the doorway and lowers his voice: 'With a great deal of difficulty, I can tell you; but with a clean conscience, too. If someone'd stopped the Grayers in an earlier decade, Miss Timms, my nephew and your sister'd still be with us. But nobody did. 'Cause nobody knew this backstory. But *I* know, and *I'm* trying to stop them. This is war. In war, ends justify means. War *is* ends justifying means. And believe it or not, I'm a secret warrior in this invisible war. So yes –' a glob of saliva flies from his lips '– I make no apology for combing through Sally's doctors' notes from both Singapore and Great Malvern, and by adding two and two—'

Hang on – 'Sally didn't see a therapist in Malvern. She loved it there.'

The pity in the old man's face is disturbingly genuine: 'She was miserable, Miss Timms. The bullying was merciless. She wanted to die.'

'No,' I'm saying, 'no way. She would've told me. We're family.'

'Often as not,' Fred Pink scratches his thigh, 'the family's the last to know about the big stuff. Wouldn't you agree?'

I can't work out if he's referring to my complex sexuality. Fred Pink may be sporadically insane, but he's no fool. I sip my tonic water and find my glass is empty. 8.57. I should just go. Now. Really.

'You're an Engifted too, see.' Fred Pink gazes at my forehead. 'Call it an aura, call it a feeling, but I know you're humming with psychovoltage yourself. That's why we met here and not down Slade Alley. The alley's where the Grayers' aperture opens, into their orison. They'd sniff you out.'

I've met enough delusionals to know they have answers for every logical objection – that's why they're delusionals – but I ask this: 'If these "soul vampires" only wanted Sally, why abduct the other five? Where are Alan and the others now?'

'The Grayers didn't want any witnesses. Alan and the others, they were just . . .' Fred Pink clenches his face again, as if in pain. 'Snuffed out. Their bodies were chucked into the gap between the orison and our world. Like bin bags down a garbage chute. The only upside is, their souls moved on while Sally's was . . . converted. Eaten.'

Maybe a part of me thinks logic can still save Fred

Pink, or maybe I've a morbid curiosity about his psychosis, or maybe it's both. 'And why didn't the police ever investigate this Slade House, if it's so near to where Sally and Alan vanished?'

'Slade House was bombed to rubble in 1940. Direct hit by a German bomb. Cranbury Avenue and Westwood Road were built over it after the war.'

It's 8.59. 'So how was Sally lured in in 1997?'

'She was lured into an *orison* of Slade House. A copy. A shadow theatre. For pre-surgery.'

'And why weren't the Grayers' preserved bodies in their attic lacuna destroyed by the bomb?'

''Cause *in* the lacuna, it's always a few minutes after 11 p.m. on Saturday, 27 October, 1934. The very second the lacuna went live, so to speak. If you'd been there watching, you'd've seen the Grayers vanish, *whoosh*, like you'd just glimpsed them from a fast train hurtling by at the speed of time, so to speak. But inside the lacuna, it's that moment eternally. Safer than the deepest nuclear vault under the Colorado Rockies.'

Maggs the landlady downstairs is right. I'm feeding a sad and broken old man's madness. My phone buzzes again. The clock's hands move to nine. I hear Maggs laugh long and hard; the sound reminds me of the stabbing violins from the shower scene in *Psycho*. 'Well, it's certainly a detailed, consistent theory. But . . .'

'It's a load o' codswallop, right?' Fred Pink flicks his brandy glass. It pings.

I switch off my recorder. 'I don't believe in magic, Mr Pink.'

The old man exhales a long wavery tuneless note until his lungs are empty. 'Pity, you being a journalist and all. I was hoping you'd write a big exposé for *Spyglass*. Alert the authorities.' He looks at the dark window. 'What proof'd convince you?'

'Proof that *is* proof, not faith masquerading as proof.'

'Ah.' He idly examines his ink- and tobacco-stained fingernails. I'm glad he's taking rejection this calmly. 'Proof, faith. Those words, eh?'

'I'm sorry I can't believe you, Mr Pink. Really. But I don't, and now my partner's expecting me at home.'

He nods. 'Well, I promised I'd call you a taxi, so that's what I'll do. A lunatic I may be, but I'm still a man of my word.' He stands up. 'Shan't be a tick. Check your texts. Someone's worried.'

It's over. I feel empty. Avril's sent no fewer than six messages.

U finished yet honey?
Cooked pumpkin soup

Soup will be perfect before I go to bed. Next up:

last london train from ur end:
twelve past midnite. U on it?

That's thoughtful of Avril, but it's a bit odd, considering it's only 9 p.m. Unless that 'U' means 'Will u be'. I open her third text:

ok am officially worried, tried to call,
UNAVAILABLE message. where r u?
U staying at hotel or wot? CALL xA

A hotel? Avril's not one of life's habitual worriers; why do I need a hotel? And if she can text, why can't she call? Is it the network? The next text reads:

Hon its 3am and I know ur big tuff girl
but CALL to say ur ok or I wont sleep.
Lotta's wedding 2moro u rmmbr?

3 a.m. ? What's she on about? My mobile's saying 21.02; the cracked clock agrees. She never gets rat-arsed on drink and she never smokes dope. I call her mobile . . . and get a NO SIGNAL DETECTED message. Fantastic. Vodafone must have begun upgrading their network after Avril's texts arrived. I scroll down to message five:

Freya u angry? if so dnt undrstnd
sorry, cldnt sleep cnt think worried
sick. Lottas wedding begins noon
dnt know if I shd go or call police
or wot. dont care what happnd or
if u with anyone but pls PLS call.

Avril doesn't do head-screwing jokes like this, but if it isn't a joke, it's a mental meltdown. 'If u with anyone'? We're monogamous. We have been since day one. Avril knows that. She should know that. I try calling our neighbour, Tom, but it's still NO SIGNAL DETECTED. Maybe there's a payphone in the bar – The Fox and Hounds is pretty much stuck in the 1980s. Otherwise I'll ask Maggs the Moody Cow if I can pay to use her landline. I read the final text:

> told Lotta u have glandular fever
> so we stay at home. called Nic n
> Beryl but they not hear from u.
> police say wait 48 hrs b4 search.
> PLS FREYA CALL ME, AM
> LOSING MY MIND!!!

Nothing Fred Pink has said tonight disturbs me as much as this. Avril's the sane one who soothes away my nightmares; who reattaches my handle when I fly off it. The only explanation is that, yes indeed, she has lost her mind. I hurry down the steep stairs to the bar below . . .

. . . and when I arrive, I enter the upstairs room I just left . . . and I stand there gasping and shuddering, as if I've just been drenched in icy water. My hand grips the doorframe. The same tables, the same chairs, the same nighttime window, the same enamelled Guinness ad with a leprechaun playing a fiddle: the *up*stairs room of The Fox and Hounds. By going *down* I went *up*. My brain insists this happened. My brain insists this can't have happened. My digital recorder's still on the table we were sitting at – I forgot to pick it up in my panic – between my undrunk tomato juice, my empty cashew nut packets, and Fred Pink's brandy glass. Behind me, the stairs are going *down*, and I can see the floor of the bar below, an ugly chessboard pattern. I hear the *Have I Got News for You* theme tune from the TV. *Breathe, Freya; think*. Stress does this; your job is stressful; hearing a nutter tell you your sister had her soul converted into diesel was stressful. Avril's texts were stressful. Memory's a slippery eel at the best of times, so obviously, *ob*viously, you just, just 'pre-imagined' going downstairs but didn't actually go. If you walk down the stairs again – I mean now – one calm step at a time, I'm sure—

My phone rings. Fumblingly, I get it out of my handbag; the screen says CALLER NOT RECOGNISED. I fire off a fierce secular prayer that it's Avril and answer with a frantic 'Hello?'

All I hear is an uncoiling sandstorm of static.

I speak at it: 'This is Freya Timms. Who's this?'

Maybe standing by the window will strengthen the signal.

I speak more loudly and clearly: 'Avril? Is that you?'

Big trees on Westwood Road smother streetlamps.

Deep inside the static, words form: '*Please! I can't breathe!*'

Sally. Sally. It's Sally. I'm crouching on the floor. My sister.

It can't be; it *is*; listen! '*You can't do this to me — you can't!*'

My sister's alive! Hurt and scared, but alive! My words unblock and my tight throat opens enough to say, 'It's Freya, Sal — where are you? Sal! Where are you?'

The static howls and beats and flaps and wails and thrashes and I hear '*Someone'llstopyouonedayyou'llsufferyou'll pay—*'

The line's dead, the screen says NO SIGNAL DETECTED and in my head I'm screaming *NO!* but that won't help so I'm clicking through the menus to CALL REGISTER but I hit GAMES and activate Snake and my stupid bastard phone won't let me go back until it's all loaded, but Sal's alive alive alive, and I should call the police now, but what if she calls back when I'm talking to them, or what if she's been locked in a psycho's cellar for nine years like that Kampusch woman in Austria who escaped from her captor a couple of months ago or what if—

My phone's trilling and flashing. I answer: 'Sally!'

'No, dearie. This is the Moody Cow from downstairs.'

Maggs the landlady? 'Look, I'm coming down, I need—'

'It's a bit late to help Sally now, I'm afraid, dearie.'

I hear her say the line one more time in my head.

I can't speak, or move, or think, or do anything at all . . .

. . . the dead flies in the strip-light have woken up.

'That was only her echo, dearie. Her residue. Time's voicemail, if you like, from nine years ago. Oh, very well, then — it was your sister's ghost talking.'

182

Fear shunts me back through gluey air. 'Who are you?'

Maggs sounds teasing and friendly: 'Surely one of *Spyglass* magazine's top journalists could hazard an intelligent guess after everything you've heard this evening?'

What have I missed? 'Let me speak with Mr Pink.'

'The real Fred passed away months ago, dearie. Prostate cancer. A horrible way to go.'

A deep gulp inflates my lungs: a *bona fide* psychopath who impersonates the dead and keeps a fan club of sicko helpers – the other customers? A locked-up pub; blinds down; murder. *Murder*. I go to the window. It's a sash design, but it has frame locks and it won't open.

The landlady's voice crackles out of my Nokia: 'Still there, are you, dearie? The connection's breaking up.'

Keep her talking: 'Look, just tell me where Sally is, I'm sure—'

'Sally's not anywhere. Sally's dead. Dead. Dead. Dead.'

I drop the phone and let it lie and grab a chair to smash the window and scream blue bloody murder and wake the street and scramble down a drainpipe or jump out but when I turn back to smash the glass the window's gone. It's wall. It's gone. It's wall . . .

. . . I turn to the stairs. The stairs are gone. There's a pale door instead, with a worn gold doorknob. The landlady's on the other side. She's doing this. I don't know how, but she's doing this, and she's inside my head. Or wait wait wait—

I'm doing it. *I'm* the one with the psychosis, not Fred Pink.

I need an ambulance, not a police car. 999. Dial it. Now.

Really, which is likelier? The laws of physics breaking down, or a stressed-out journalist breaking down? I pick up my phone, praying this lucidity lasts. A crisp, efficient-sounding lady answers straight off: 'Hello, emergency services?'

'Yeah, hi, I – my name's Freya Timms, I – I – I – I —'

'Calm yourself, Freya.' The operator sounds like my mum, but efficient. 'Tell me the situation and we'll see what we can do to help.'

If I speak about hallucinations in pubs, she'll fob me off with a helpline number. I need something drastic: 'I've gone into labour; I'm on my own, but I'm in a wheelchair, and I need an ambulance.'

'That's fine, Freya, don't worry; what's your location?'

'A pub – The Fox and Hounds, but I'm not from around here so—'

'It's fine, Freya, I know The Fox and Hounds. My brother and I live just down the street.'

I think, *Thank God!* but then I understand.

I understand why she just sounded so amused.

I understand there's no way out of here.

'Better late than never,' says the stern voice on the phone. 'Turn around and look at the candle on the table, behind you. Now.'

As I obey, the room dims. A candle sits on an ornate

candlestick engraved with runes on its stem and base. The flame sways.

'Watch the flame,' orders the voice. '*Watch.*'

Reality folds in, origamilike, and darkens to black. I can't feel my body but I'm kneeling, I think, and three faces have joined me. Left of the candle hovers a woman in her mid-thirties. She's familiar . . . it's Maggs the landlady, but twenty years younger, slimmer, blonder, smoother-skinned and eerily beautiful. Right of the candle is a man of the same age, also blond, and also known to me . . . as I study him, a young Fred Pink emerges from his face. The two are twins. Who can they be but Norah and Jonah Grayer? They are absolutely motionless, like the candle flame, and like the third face watching me over the candle. Freya Timms staring out of a mirror. I try to move a limb, a thumb, an eyelid, but my nervous system has shut down. Is this what happened to Sal? I suspect the answer is yes. Did she think of me? Did she want her big sister to come and rescue her? Or was she past that stage by then?

'Unbelievable!' Norah Grayer's face flickers into fury as the candle's flame untwists and twists. Maybe I've been here minutes, maybe days. Time needs time to be measurable. 'How *dare* you?'

'Sister.' Jonah Grayer swivels his jaw as if it fits poorly. Me, I'm still paralysed from the eyeballs down.

'You told our entire life story to this wretched reporter!'

'Fred Pink had to share *some* of his findings, or the Oink's sister would've decided he was wasting her time and cleared off prematurely. Why the hysteria?'

'Don't "hysteria" me!' Spittle flies over the candle. 'For even *naming* the Shaded Way, the Sayyid would nullify you. On the spot and with just cause!'

'Oh, I'd like to see the Sayyid *try*, peace be upon him. What are you afraid of? Our story's a banquet of marvels, and it's exactly *never* that the chance comes along to share it with a discreet listener. Because she *is* discreet. Shall we ask her how discreet she is? Let's. It'll put your mind at rest.' He turns to me. 'Miss Timms: do you intend to publish Fred Pink's backstory, as you heard it told on this memorable evening?'

I can't shake – or nod – my head by so much as a millimetre.

'We can take that as a no, Sister dear. Just chill.'

'"Chill"? So *acting* like a teenager is no longer enough? Our guest was damn nearly a no-show; she rejected the first banjax and—'

'No no no no no. No, Norah. You're doing it again – scaring yourself with all manner of what ifs instead of acknowledging an entirely successful outcome.'

What's happening? I am desperate to ask. What outcome?

'Fred Pink told you all the answers, honey pie,' Jonah

turns his mocking face my way, 'but I'll spell it out for you, since your sister evidently inherited the brains as well as the puppy fat. On your way to meet me – me, in a random old man's body which I commandeered to be Mr Pink – you decided that our rendezvous was a waste of time after all. Having planned for this eventuality, I had you followed, and at a sheltered bend in the park near the bandstand, one of my Blackwatermen sprayed an ingenious compound in your face. You lost consciousness on the spot, poor thing. Thanks to my fastidious foresight –' he glances at his sister '– a St John ambulance was only a minute away. Our worthy volunteers had you safe, sound, strapped in a wheelchair and brought to our aperture within five short minutes. My men even hid your face under a hood, to protect you from the spots of rain. And from prying eyes. You were rendered into our orison, which my sister had swiftly redesigned into a rough copy of The Fox and Hounds – your original destination – and brought to the orison's heart, the lacuna. Given the difficulties of redacting memories from an Engifted mind, I played safe and wiped out the whole day, which is why you can't remember leaving London this afternoon. When you awoke, I treated you to the greatest scoop of your life. There.' Jonah runs his tongue along his upper teeth. 'Wasn't that satisfying? I feel like a detective laying out the facts in the final scene of a whodunnit. Yes, yes, Sister,' Jonah turns once more to his sister, who still looks furious, 'our guest turned up her nose at the tomato juice, but we banjaxed her good and proper with the cashew nuts. And yes, I went off script a smidgeon during my turn as Fred Pink and revealed a little more than I'd meant to; but she'll be dead in two minutes, and dead journalists don't file copy.'

Dead? He did say 'dead'? They're going to kill me?

'You were a fool and a braggart, Brother.' Norah's voice is hard with anger, but I'm only half hearing. '*Never* discuss la Voie Ombragée with anyone. Nor Ely, Swaffham, Cantillon, nor Aït Arif. Ever. Whatever the circumstances. *Ever.*'

'I'll do my best to mend my ways, Sister dear.' Jonah gives a mock-contrite sigh.

Norah's disgusted. 'One day your flippancy will kill you.'

'If you say so, Sister.'

'And on that day I will save myself if I can, and abandon you if I must.'

Jonah's about to reply – perhaps with a smarmy retort – but changes his mind and the subject. 'I am famished, you are famished, our operandi is famished and supper is plucked, trussed, seasoned and' – he turns his whole body to face me and whispers – 'bewitched, bothered and bewildered. You're not breathing, honey pie. Have you really not noticed?'

I want this to be a sadistic lie but it's true – I'm not breathing. So this is it. I don't die in crossfire, or in a car crash, or at sea, but here, inside this . . . nightmare that can't be real, but which, nonetheless, is. The twins begin to pluck and ply the space in front of them, slowly at first, then faster. Now they seem to draw on the air, like high-speed calligraphers. Their lips move too, but I don't know if I'm hearing my captors or if it's the buzzing echoes of my oxygen-starved brain closing down. Above the candle, a thing congeals into being. It's the size of a misshapen head, but faceless. It glows, red, bright to dark, bright to dark, and stringy roots emerge from its sides and underbelly, fixing it in the dark air. Longer roots snake their way towards me. I try to squirm my head back or shut my eyes but I can't. I'd scream if I could, a loud, hard, horror-film scream, but I can't. The roots twist into my mouth, nose and ears, and then I feel a spear-tip of pain where my Cyclops eye would be. Something is being extracted through the same spot; it comes into focus a few inches from my eyes, a translucent shimmering globe, smaller than a billiard ball, but cloudy with countless stars. It's my true me. It's my soul. The Grayer twins lean in.

They purse their lips and inhale, sharply.

My soul distends like a thick-walled bubble being pulled apart.

It's mine, it's me, but it's hopeless, it's hopeless, it's hope—

Suddenly, a figure fills the narrow gap between the Grayers, blocking my view. She's a she, in a designer jacket. Her plump midriff blocks what little light shines from the candle and the heart-brain-thing above it. Norah Grayer falls back to my right, shock twisting her face. Jonah can't move away, even if he wanted to: one of the intruder's small hands – she has peacock-blue fingernails – grips his neck, while the other hand, swift as a bird's wing, plunges a thick, six-inch needle into one side of his windpipe and clean out of the other, like a cocktail stick piercing a very large olive. Blood seeps from both punctures, treacle-black on stone-grey in this dimness. Jonah's eyes bulge in disbelief, his head and jaw slump and his two puncture wounds froth as he tries to make a noise. His attacker releases him, but the weapon – a hairpin, if I'm not wrong – stays jammed in place. As his head tilts, I have a view of a silver fox's head with gemstone eyes at the top of the hairpin. Shouted fragments reach me from Norah, a few feet and light years away – *Get out! Damn ghost! GET OUT!* The intruder is fading away now – I see the candle flame through her body. My stretched soul has reformed itself into a single globe and is now fading away too. My body is dead but my soul is saved. My rescuer's pendant swings through my soul, lit deep-sea green by the last of the starry atoms. Eternity, jade, it's Maori, I chose it, I wrapped it, I sent it once to someone I love.

ASTRONAUTS

2015

Bombadil's iPhone vibrates over his heart. With his cold fingers, I fish out the device from the large skiing jacket I had him buy near our anonymous hotel this morning when I saw the ominous state of the sky. Sleet peppers the screen. The message is from the Blackwaterman:

yr guest parked 50m from Westwood Road
entrance to alley, navy blue VW Tiguan.

I reply concisely:

good news

Our operatives are masters of their martial craft and need no further orders. I half feared the wintry weather might delay our guest, or even deter her from making the car journey altogether. Turning a no-show into a show would have complicated the day in tense, unpleasant ways, but instead our guest is a quarter of an hour early and we can afford to relax a little. On a whim, I locate Philip

Glass's music for *The Truman Show* on Bombadil's iPhone, and listen to it by way of pre-prandial entertainment. Jonah and I saw the film at a backstreet cinema in St Tropez at the turn of the century. We were moved by the protagonist's horror at discovering the breadth and depth of the gulf between his own life and the quotidian world. Now I think of it, the Côte d'Azur could be the right sanctuary for Jonah to spend a few weeks after nine static years in his wounded body. The Riviera has no lack of privileged hosts whose hair Jonah could let down, and I would enjoy the sunshine on a host's skin after five days of this absurd English weather. A moon-grey cat appears at Bombadil's feet, meowing for food. 'You're not as hungry as we are,' I assure it. The wind slams down Slade Alley, flurrying sleet and leaves in its roiling coil. I zip up Bombadil's hood to protect his earphones, restricting my view to a fur-lined oval, and think of sandstorms at the Sayyid's house in the Atlas Mountains. How the twentieth century hurtled away. The cat has given me up as a lost cause. Bombadil's toes are numb in his flimsy trainers, but he'll be dead before his chilblains can bloom. My conscience rests easy.

And here comes our guest. A short, slim figure, bulked out by cold-weather clothing, walks down Slade Alley, backlit by sleet-white, hurrying light. Dr Iris Marinus-Fenby is a psychiatrist from Toronto on a placement at Dawkins Hospital, outside Slough. Two twists of fate set her on the path that has delivered her to our aperture. The first is that in 2008 she obtained the notebooks of Fred Pink, the former Dawkins patient who died in 2005. She wrote a series of academic papers on abduction psychoses, drawing from the notebooks, in which she describes Pink's obsession with Jonah and Norah Grayer, a pair of long-dead 'soul vampires'. The second twist of fate is that Iris Marinus-Fenby is, against quite delicious odds, an Engifted herself, and is therefore fair game. The Mighty Shrink proved absurdly easy to lure here. She stops a few paces away; a black professional in her late thirties – a smooth, sub-Saharan, black-leather-jacket black that sharpens the whites of her eyes and teeth. Marinus-Fenby dresses dowdily for work, and even off duty she hides her figure under mannish clothes: a sheepskin flying jacket, rumpled trousers, hiking boots, a moss-green beret, a keffiyeh round her neck and little or no make-up. She wears her wiry hair short. A khaki canvas bag is tucked under her shoulder. Calmly, she sizes up Bombadil, a skinny Caucasian in his early twenties, with bad skin, an ill-advised lip-stud, a sharkish chin, a cheesy smell, and sore eyes. My host is swallowed up by his XXL ski jacket. Iris Marinus-Fenby, PhD, sees her next research subject, her Fred Pink the Second, and this one, she gets to meet in the flesh. I unplug Bombadil from his headphones and have him give our guest a *Got a problem?* face.

She recites the first line of the word-key: 'Yes, I'm looking for a pub called The Green Man.' Her voice is deep, clear and has an accent that used to be labelled 'mid-Atlantic'.

Bombadil speaks with a nervous mutter that I do not modify: 'No. The Green Man's gone the way of The Fox and Hounds.'

Iris Marinus-Fenby offers her gloved hand. 'Bombadil.'

I feel the prickle of psychovoltage, even through her cashmere gloves. 'Dr Iris Marinus-Fenby.'

'Nine syllables wears you out. "Marinus" is fine.'

I notice the blue checks of her keffiyeh are in fact tiny Stars of David. What a smug piece of symbolism. Our handshake ends. 'Isn't that, like, calling you by your surname?'

The Mighty Shrink duly notes my nomenclatural sensitivities: 'Marinus is more of an inner name than a family name.'

I have Bombadil shrug. 'Welcome back to Slade Alley, Marinus.'

'Thanks for reaching out to me.' She knows better than to ask for my real name. 'Your emails were fascinating.'

'Thought it'd broaden your mind, seeing a real live orison, like.'

'I'm very curious about what we'll see, Bombadil. Say, this wind's sharp as a razor. Would you prefer to talk where it's warmer? My car's parked just on the street, or there's a Starbucks at the Green. Did you have lunch already? I'm buying.'

'I never talk where I haven't swept for wires,' I tell her.

Marinus makes a mental note of this. 'I understand.'

I nod along the alley. 'Let's jump in at the deep end, like.'

'Go straight inside the "orison", you mean?'

'Yup. Still there. I went in yesterday, too.'

'So that's once on Thursday as well as yesterday? Two visits in total?'

'One and one is two.' I nod, amused by her professional demeanour. 'They don't happen along very often.'

'And the way in, into the "aperture", it's still –' she looks down the claustrophobic middle section of Slade Alley '– down here?'

'Sure is, Doc. Exactly where *you* said Fred Pink wrote that Gordon Edmonds said he found it, all those years ago.'

Marinus marvels that this gawky geeky English boy reads the *American Journal of Psychiatry*. 'Lead the way.'

Twenty paces later we stop at the aperture, and for the first time our guest is flummoxed. 'It's small, it's black, it's iron.' I enjoy spelling out the obvious. 'Exactly as Fred Pink described it.'

Marinus touches it. 'There wasn't a door here three years ago.'

'There wasn't a door here three *days* ago. But when I did my post-dawn recce on Thursday morning, voilà.'

Marinus looks up and down the alley, then crouches down to inspect the sides. 'Looks as if it's been here for years. This is odd. Check out the lichen, this scuffed concrete . . .'

'Apertures are chameleons, Doc. They blend in.'

She looks at me, her faith in a logical explanation shaken but as yet intact. 'What's on the other side?'

'That's the cool bit. Look *over* the wall with a twelve-foot ladder, you see this . . .' I have Bombadil produce a photo from an inner pocket. 'The back garden of a semi-detached house, built in 1952, home to Jamal and Sue al-Awi and their two point four children – literally, she's in her second trimester, according to her hospital records. But if you go *through* the aperture –' I rap the soundless surface with my knuckles '– you'll find the terraced garden of Slade House, as it appeared in the 1930s, on a foggy, mild day.'

Marinus gives me an assessing look.

'The fog was a total surprise,' I tell her.

Marinus is wishing she was recording all this. 'You mean the same Slade House that got razed in the Blitz, in 1940?'

'December twentieth, 1940. Just in time for Christmas. Yes.'

'So are you saying this door's a kind of . . . time-portal?'

'No, no, no, that's a classic beginner's mistake. An aperture's a portal into an orison. A reality bubble. God, I wish you could see your face right now, Doc.'

The Mighty Shrink looks shifty *and* puzzled. 'I have faith that *you* believe, Bombadil, but science requires proof. As you know.'

'And proof requires reliable witnesses,' I have Bombadil answer, 'ideally with PhDs.' The wind bounces a plastic bottle off the floor and walls of the alley. We stand aside to let it pass. Tall weeds sway.

Marinus raps her knuckles on the aperture. 'No sound when you hit it. The metal's warm, too, for such a cold day. How do you open it? There's no keyhole.'

I have Bombadil do a zipped-up smile. 'Mind power.'

Marinus waits for me to explain, shivering despite her cold-weather clothes.

'Visualise the keyhole,' I elaborate, 'visualise the key, visualise inserting the key, turning it, and the door opening. If you know what you're about, that's how you pass though an aperture.'

Marinus nods gravely to assure me she doesn't disbelieve me. This woman's amusing. 'And when you went inside, what did you do there?'

'On Thursday, I didn't dare leave the shrubbery I found on the other side. I learned to be a bit cautious after my last orison in New Mexico. So I just sat there for ten minutes, watching, then came back out again. Yesterday, I was braver. Walked up as far as a big ginkgo tree – not that I knew what it was, but I brought a leaf back and looked it up. I've got an app.'

Marinus, of course, asks, 'Do you still have this leaf?'

I have Bombadil hand her a zip-up freezer bag.

She holds it up: 'Yes, that's a ginkgo leaf.' She doesn't add that the leaf could have come from anywhere. 'Did you take any photos on the inside?'

I puff out Bombadil's near-frozen cheeks. 'Tried. Took about fifty on Thursday on my phone, but on the way back they all got wiped. Yesterday I took in my old Nikon and shot off a reel but when I developed it last night – blank. No surprise, to be honest: of the five astronauts I've met who are the real deal, not one has ever returned from an expedition with a single photo or video clip intact. There's something about orisons. They refuse to be recorded, like.'

'"Astronauts"?'

'It's what we call ourselves. It's online misdirection. "Orison tourist" or something like that'd attract the wrong sort of attention.'

Marinus hands back the freezer bag. 'So astronauts can bring samples of flora out but not images?'

I have Bombadil shrug. 'I don't make the laws, Doc.'

Behind a wall, someone's bouncing on a squeaky trampoline.

'Did you see any signs of life?' asks Marinus. 'Inside the orison, I mean.'

The Mighty Shrink still thinks she's studying a psychiatric phenomenon, not an ontological one. I can be patient: she'll learn. 'Blackbirds. Plus a squirrel – cute and red, not grey and ratty – and fish in a pond. But no people. The curtains in Slade House stayed drawn and the door stayed shut, and nobody's used the aperture since four o'clock on Thursday.'

'You sound very sure.'

'I am.' I touch a brick opposite the aperture. 'See this?'

The Mighty Shrink straightens up and looks. 'It's a brick.'

The trampoliner's giggling his head off. He's a young boy.

'No. It's the facia of a brick, bonded onto a steel-framed box containing a webcam, a power-pack and a sensor to switch the lens to infra-red. What the camera sees through *this* two-mil hole' – I point – 'feeds straight to my phone.'

I show Marinus my iPhone. Its screen shows me showing Marinus my iPhone.

She's duly impressed. 'A neat bit of kit. You built it yourself?'

'Yeah, but full credit to the Israelis – I hacked the specs from Mossad.' I give my spy-brick – installed by the Blackwatermen earlier today – a friendly pat and turn back to the aperture. 'So. All set for the great adventure?'

Marinus hesitates, wondering how I'll react when my own private fantasy island fails to materialise. Scientific curiosity trumps caution. 'I'll follow in your footsteps, Bombadil.'

I kneel before the aperture and place a palm on it. Its warmth is pleasant on Bombadil's icy hand, and Jonah becomes telegrammable: *Brother, our guest has arrived – I presume everything's ready?*

Look who it isn't. His signal is weak. *I thought you'd buggered off to a 'retreat' in Kirishima again . . .*

Give me strength. *No, Jonah – it's Open Day, and our metalives depend on my being* here, *and your having the orison and sub-orison ready.*

Jonah sniffs telegrammatically. *Well, it's very kind of you to bother visiting your incarcerated brother.*

I visited you yesterday, I remind him. *My trip to Kirishima was six* years *ago – and I was only gone for thirteen months.*

A grumpy pause unwinds: *Thirteen months is thirteen eternities if you're stuck in a lacuna. I would never have deserted you, were the shoe on the other foot.*

I shoot back: *Like the time you didn't desert me in Antarctica for two whole years? For a 'joke'? Or the time you didn't forget me on the Society Islands while you went 'yachting' with your Scientologist friends?*

Another grumpy Jonah pause. *Your birth-body didn't have a hairpin stuck through its throat.*

After nearly twelve decades together, I know better than to feed my brother's self-pity: *Nor would yours now if you'd heeded my warnings about the operandi's aberrations.* Our guest is waiting and Bombadil's body is shivering. *I'm opening the aperture on the count of three, so unless you fancy committing suicide* and *fratricide in a single fit of pique, project the garden now. One . . . two . . .*

I slip Bombadil's body through first. All's well. The Mighty Shrink follows, expecting a poky backyard but finding herself at the foot of a long, stepped garden rising to a pencilled-on-fog Slade House. Iris Marinus-Fenby, MD, straightens up slowly, her eyes as astonished as her jaw is drooping. I have Bombadil do a taut giggle. Our operandi is utterly depleted, so Jonah has only a glimmer of voltage to project today's orison, but it won't need to bedazzle or seduce the senses like the Hallowe'en party or the policeman's honey-trap: this orison's mere existence is enough to render Marinus pliable. I clear Bombadil's throat. 'Is this proof yet, Doc?'

Marinus can only point, weakly, towards the house.

'Uh-huh. A big house. Large as life. As real as we are.'

Our guest turns to the aperture, hidden by camellias. 'Don't worry. It's stable. We won't get locked in.'

The Cautious Shrink crouches and peers back out into Slade Alley. My phone is ready to call the Blackwatermen, but Marinus soon comes back, takes off her beret and puts her beret back on, just to buy a little time, I think. 'I found an old postcard, in Fred Pink's notes,' she says in a faltering voice. 'Of Slade House. That' – she looks at the old rectory – 'that's it. But . . . I *checked* the council archives, Ordnance Survey, Google Street View. Slade House isn't here. And even if it were, there's no space for it to fit between Westwood Road and Cranbury Avenue. It's not here. It can't be. But it's here.'

'It's a conundrum, I agree, unless Fred Pink was,' I whisper, 'y'know, Doc . . . *right*. As in, not bug-fuck crazy after all.'

A pigeon is heard but not seen in the damson trees.

Marinus looks at me to see if I heard it too.

I can't help but have Bombadil smile. 'A pigeon.'

Marinus bites her thumb and examines the bite mark.

'It's not a dream,' I tell her. ' You're insulting the orison.'

Marinus plucks a camellia leaf, bites that and examines it.

She lobs a stone at the sundial. It smacks it, stonily.

Marinus presses her hand on the dewy grass. It leaves a print. 'Holy hell.' She looks at me. 'It's all real, isn't it?'

'In its local, enclosed, pocket, bubble, orison way. Yes.'

The Mighty Shrink stands up again, puts her hands together as if in prayer, covers her nose and mouth for a few seconds, then shoves her hands into her flying jacket. 'My patients at Dawkins, in Toronto, in Vancouver . . . my abductee-fantasists . . . were they all . . . in fact – *right*? For, for, for experiencing *this*, did I, did I – did I sign off on restraint orders and dose them to the gills with anti-psychotic drugs?'

We're at a delicate stage. I need to coax Marinus up to the house without her either sensing a trap, or being crushed by remorse, or being spooked into running for the exit. 'Look, real orisons are rare. Less than a single per cent of your patients are authentic astronauts. The others, no – they needed the drugs, they needed your help. Get down off that cross, Doc. It's not for you.'

'One per cent is still . . . too many.' Marinus bites her lower lip and shakes her head. 'So much for "First, do no harm".'

'Orisons aren't covered at medical college. Sure, you'll never get this printed in peer review journals, like, but if you want to help your patients, look around. Explore. Observe. You're a flexible thinker. That's why I chose you.'

Marinus lets my words sink in. She takes a few steps over the lawn, looking up at the blank wet white sky. 'Fred Pink – who until two minutes ago, I – I thought was delusional – Fred Pink thought Slade House was dangerous. Is it?'

I have Bombadil unzip his ski jacket. 'I don't think so, no.'

'But we – Christ, I can't believe I'm saying this – we just stepped from our reality into another. Didn't we?'

I feign mild disappointment at Marinus's timidity. 'We're

astronauts; and yeah, it's a riskier hobby than collecting Lego figurines. Now as it happens, I strongly suspect Slade House is a deserted orison running on autopilot and nobody's set foot here for a very long time. But, if you'd feel safer going back to your consultancy at Dawkins, dosing up future Fred Pinks on Izunolethe and antidepressants and whatever and visiting them in padded cells, knowing that *you* were the first and last clinical psychiatrist to chicken out of exploring a real live orison, then who could blame you? Have a safe drive home, Doc.' I walk off towards the sundial.

'Bombadil.' Marinus's footsteps hurry after me. 'Wait!' Her professional conscience is a collar. I hold the leash.

Droplets of mist cling to the lavender. Lavender, I remember, was one of the happier scents of Jonah's and my childhood on the Swaffham estate in Norfolk, where the Chetwynd-Pitts' tenant farmers grew several acres of the flowers for the London perfumeries. I pause while Marinus pinches and sniffs. 'Smells like the real thing,' she says, 'but why's everything turning black and white? The camellias were red and pink but this lavender's grey. Those roses are monochrome.'

I know exactly why: after eighteen years without fresh voltage, our operandi is now too drained to sustain colour reliably. 'Decay,' I answer with a half-truth 'I'm more sure than ever the Grayer twins have gone for good. The fog's another sign. We can relax a little, Doc. We're visiting a ruin.'

Looking reassured, Marinus unwinds her keffiyeh. 'Human beings created this place? Every pebble, every twig, every droplet of mist, every blade of grass? Every atom?' She shakes her head. 'It's like . . . a divine act.'

'I'd lay off the particle physics, Doc, if I were you. But yeah, it's people and not gods, if that's what you're getting at. If it helps, think of orisons as set designs for a theatre. Careful, a bramble's got you.'

Marinus unpicks it from the hem of her coat. 'Ouch. The thorns are real, too. How many of these places have you visited?'

I draw on Bombadil's genuine experiences. 'This is number three. First was on the island of Iona, in the Scottish Hebrides. Quite a well-known orison, that one. Relatively, anyway, like. It was awesome. It's an apse in the abbey that's not there unless you know where and when to slip through a certain archway. The time disparity was *chronic*, mind. When I got back after only a day away, two whole years'd passed and Mum'd got remarried to a divorced Microsoft rep.'

'That's' – the Mighty Shrink searches for words – 'incredible.'

'I frickin' know it's incredible! *Microsoft*! My second orison was more hardcore. Its aperture was in a high school for the arts in Santa Fe. Yoyo, an astronaut from Cedar Rapids, tracked it down. It was in a cleaning cupboard.'

Marinus asks, 'What makes a "hardcore" orison different from the one on Iona, or this one?'

'Unhappy endings. Yoyo never came out.'

Marinus stops. 'He *died* in there?'

'Well, no, he chose to stay inside – and he's still there, as far as I know – but its creator *was* in residence and he had a bad-ass Jehovah complex. Named his little world Milk and Honey. When I wanted to leave he accused me of apostasy and tried to, uh, kill me. 'Nother story, all that. But all *this'* – I have Bombadil gesture about us – 'peace and quiet is a world away from that. Look, wild strawberries.' The straw-berries are the banjax that Jonah and I agreed to feed our guest. If I can get Marinus to eat one now, it'll save having to create a sub-orison inside the house. I pick a couple of the fatter fruits and pop one into my mouth. 'Juicy. Try one.'

Marinus's hand begins to rise; but drops down. 'Maybe not.'

Damn it. Damn her. I have Bombadil grin. 'Scared?'

The Mighty Shrink looks cagey. 'Mildly superstitious. In all the tales, the myths, the rule is, if you eat or drink anything – pomegranate seeds, faerie wine, whatever – the place has a hold on you.'

Inwardly, I curse. '"Myths", Doc? Are myths science?'

'When I'm in doubt – as I am now – I ask myself, "What would Carl Jung do?" – and act accordingly. Call it a gut instinct.'

If I push the banjax too hard, she'll grow suspicious. Jonah will just have to muster the voltage for a sub-orison. 'Suit yourself,' I say, and eat the other strawberry. If Marinus weren't so engifted, I could have just suasioned her to eat it; but then if she weren't so engifted, she wouldn't be here. 'Awesome. You don't know what you're missing.'

The wisteria's twisted boughs are dripping with blooms, never mind that it's October in the world outside. But when Marinus reaches up to touch the flowers, her hand passes clean through. The only vivid colours left in the orison now are the dyes in the clothes we came in with. Clothes. I'm nagged by the thought that I've missed something . . . What about? Clothes – possessions – what? It was a similarly nagging thought that had tried to warn me before Sally Timms attacked Jonah nine years ago, but I didn't listen closely enough. If Jonah weren't having trouble maintaining the orison I'd telegram him to pause it so I could stop and figure out what's bothering me. As we emerge onto the upper lawn, a black and white peacock darting across our path just fades into the air, leaving a dying trail of *Cuckoo! Cuckoo! Cuckoo!* Luckily Marinus was distracted by the ginkgo tree looming up far too quickly for our cautious amble. 'This is as far as I came yesterday,' I say, and stop: thousands of fallen leaves fall upwards from the grey lawn, all at once, and attach themselves to the tree. Marinus is enchanted by the sight, but I feel a queasiness in Bombadil's stomach: this is serious malprojection, not whimsy. Jonah's losing control of the orison. 'It's like a dream in here,' says Marinus.

My brother telegrams me: *Get her inside, it's collapsing.*

Easier said than done. 'Let's look inside,' I tell our guest.

'In *there*? The house itself? Are you sure that's wise?'

'Yeah,' I have Bombadil say. 'Why ever not?'

An anxious silence is followed by a worried 'Why?'

I appeal to a force that is stronger than our guest's cowardice. 'Look, Doc, I didn't want to raise any false hopes before, but there's a chance of finding Fred Pink alive in there.' I look at the upper windows.

'Alive? After nine years? Are you sure?'

Are you inside yet, Sister? telegrams Jonah. *Hurry!*

'There are no certainties when it comes to orisons, Doc,' I reply. 'But time ran differently in the Iona orison, and Milk and Honey was habitable, so I think it's possible. Don't we owe it to Fred Pink to give the place the once-over at least? It's the clues he left you that brought us here today, after all.'

The Guilty Shrink takes the bait. 'Then, yes. If there's even a chance of finding him alive, let's go.' Marinus strides over the last lawn towards Slade House, but when she looks back at me she looks past me and her eyes go wide: 'Bombadil!'

I turn around and see the end of the garden is erasing itself.

'What *is* it?' asks Marinus. 'How do we get out?'

A curved wall of nothing is uncreating the garden as the orison collapses in on itself. I thought that by finding a guest as voltaically rich as Marinus and bringing her here, my brother, our lacuna and the operandi were as good as saved. I see now that I may be too late. 'Only fog, Doc. No need to get panicky.'

'Fog? But surely . . . I mean look at how quickly it's—'

'Orison fog looks like that. Saw it in Iona, too.' I mustn't let Marinus run out into the wall of non-existence like a headless chicken. I stride on, calmly. 'Trust me, Doc. Come on. Hey – would I be this laid-back if there was anything to worry about?'

The steps up to Slade House are mossy and stained, the once-proud door is peeling and rotten and the knocker is chewed by rust and time. I open the door and hustle Marinus inside. Only thirty paces away, the ginkgo tree is being devoured by the shrinking orison. I close the door behind us and telegram Jonah, *We're in.* We hear a noise like dragged furniture and my ears pop as the orison moulds itself to the outside of the house. When I look out again through the mullioned window in the door, nothingness stares back. Blankness is a horror. 'What was that noise?' whispers Marinus.

'Thunder. The weather in here's been neglected for so long, it's all scrambled up. Fog, storms. Blazing sunshine'll be next up.'

'Oh,' says the Mighty Shrink, uncertainly. Autumn leaves are strewn over the chessboard tiles in the hallway. Our old Czech housekeeper would be appalled by this version of the Slade House she kept so spick and span in Jonah's and my corporeal days. The coving is festooned with spiderwebs, the doors are hanging off their hinges, and the panelling up the stairs is wormy and flaking. 'What now?' asks the Mighty Shrink. 'Should we search the ground floor, or—'

This time the thunder wallops the walls. They shudder. Marinus touches her ears. 'God, did you feel that?'

Brother, I telegram, *we're inside — what's wrong?*

A dying operandi is what's wrong! Jonah sounds frantic. *The house is buckling. Get the guest to the lacuna. Now.*

'It's the atmospherics,' I reassure Marinus. 'Quite normal.'

Call downstairs, I instruct Jonah.

Pregnant pause, then: *What are you talking about?*

Pretend you're Fred Pink, trapped, and call downstairs.

Another pause. Jonah asks, *What did he sound like?*

You played him last Open Day! English, gruff.

'Are you sure it's normal, Bombadil?' Marinus is afraid.

'There was a barometer in Milk and Honey,' I ad-lib, 'that—'

We hear something. Marinus holds up a finger and looks up the stairs, whispering, 'I heard someone. Did you?' I look vague and we listen. Nothing. Mile-thick nothing. Marinus begins to lower her finger, and then we hear Fred Pink's elderly, shaky voice: 'Hello? Is anyone there? Hello?'

The Fearless Shrink calls out: 'Mr Pink? Is that you?'

'Yes – yes! I – I – I – I've had a little fall. Upstairs. Please . . .'

'We'll be right with you!' Without a glance, Marinus is gone, climbing two steps at a time. For the first time since the aperture, I feel properly in control. I have Bombadil follow in Marinus's wake, relieved by how the multilingual psychiatrist with an MD – first class – from Columbus State University is so easily codded by my brother crying wolf. The carpet is threadbare, the dust has formed a light crust and when we reach the little landing, the grandfather clock is silent and its face is too scabby to read. Similarly, the portraits of our early guests are leprous with mould, and Marinus, befuddled by the strangest hour of her life, flies past them without a first glance, let alone a second. The Shrink in Shining Armour sees the pale door at the top of the stairs and launches herself up again, stepping over the desiccated body of an owl. As I pass Sally Timms' portrait, I slap her, a gesture as petty as it is pointless. She caused this trouble, or her 'ghost' did. By spiking my brother's throat at the vital second, she stopped us feeding the operandi with her sister Freya's soul, and reduced us to psychovoltaic pauperdom. Which ends today! I collide with Marinus's back, just a few steps short of the pale door, next to Freya Timms' grime-encrusted portrait, and I hiss, 'Why've you stopped, Doc?'

She's listening to the rumbling silence. 'How do we know these are the right stairs?'

I begin saying, 'Of course they are'; we hear timber splinter in the hallway below; and we hear Jonah-as-Fred Pink calling through the door above us, 'I'm in here, hello? Hello? I – I – need a little help, is anyone there? Please?' My brother's acting is as hammy as ever and the volume's too loud, but Marinus just seizes the bevelled doorknob and vanishes. On any other Open Day I would assume that the job is done and the guest is safely rendered to our lacuna in the attic, but today I assume nothing. First, I telegram, *Do you have her, Jonah?*

My answer is a bellow of splitting masonry, glass and wood as the orison's perimeter annihilates the shell of Slade House. Destruction roars up the lower stairs and Bombadil's feet are rooted to the step as my host's unconscious self and I grapple for control of his adrenalin-crazed nervous system. Through his eyes I watch the seething front of nothing reach the little landing, erase it and its dead grandfather clock, then surge up towards skinny, tattooed Bombadil. Death. Something orders me, *Jump, it's time*; but no, the operandi needs both Grayer twins, and if I obeyed the impulse, I'd kill Jonah. So I egress with a few seconds' grace, after psychoshoving Bombadil's runty body down the stairs. Thumpetty-thumpetty-thump. My ex-host yells, brokenly, his sentience returned too late to halt his descent, much less assemble his wits; and then he's gone, ski jacket, chilblains, iPhone, internet porn habit, childhood memories, body and all: gone in a non-flash. I-as-my-soul rotate and transverse through the pale door.

I emerge in a commendable copy of the private hospital room at the Royal Berkshire Hospital where I spent a recent week as a patient taking meticulous notes. True,

Marinus is a psychiatrist and not an A&E mopper-upper; true, she knows North American hospitals better than British ones; but a single anomaly could end in our guest smelling an illusory rat and rejecting the banjax, and without this anaesthetic the extraction of her soul would be messy and partial. Consequently, Jonah and I evoked the room with a fanatical eye for realism: a wall-mounted TV; a washbasin with a swivel tap; two wipeable chairs; a bedside table, a chipped vase; a door with a linen curtain over its small window; and an easy-to-read clock saying 8.01, with blinds down to suggest p.m. not a.m. The air is scented with bleach and the sonic hospital backwash includes the ping of lift doors, the trundle of trolley wheels and an unanswered phone. Dr Iris Marinus-Fenby lies unconscious with a drip in her arm and her head in a neck brace. My brother enters, evoked as himself, dressed in a doctor's white coat. He sees my soul. 'Norah. You're late.' I look at Jonah-as-Jonah, enjoying his enjoyment at moving around again, even if the movement is as illusory as the hospital room. Then I evoke myself as a senior doctor in her forties, reverting to my own voice. 'The traffic was murder.'

'Well done, Sister. How do I look?'

'Give yourself raccoon eyes and spread that indomitable jaw with some five o'clock shadow. Well done yourself.'

Jonah modifies his face and shows me his profile: 'Better?'

'Better. How are our bodies doing?'

'Yours is in a state of serene perfection, as ever; mine is still skewered through the throat with a fox-headed hairpin.

The attic walls are safe, but the operandi is a drained and dying husk, Sister. I give it fifteen minutes.'

I turn to Marinus. 'Then let's wake the patient and administer her medicine. Then we'll recharge the operandi and repair your throat, cell by cell.'

Jonah looks at the unconscious woman with impure thoughts. 'Will she offer any resistance, Sister?'

'She rejected the strawberry in the garden – citing Carl Jung and "gut instinct", if you please – but the fruit *was* the hue of raw liver, and when she wakes up she won't know if it's May Day, Marrakesh or Monteverdi. Do you have the banjax?'

Jonah evokes a red and white tablet on his palm. 'Sufficiently generic, would you say?'

'Make it smaller, so she can swallow it without effort. Have a glass of water ready. Deny her any chance to stop and think.'

Jonah shrinks the pill, tips it onto a dish and evokes a glass and a bottle of Evian on the bedside table. 'Look, when you telegrammed from the alley, I was, uh, not at my best, and—'

'You've been starved of fresh psychovoltage for eighteen years and trapped in a traumatised body for nine. I'd be insane by now, not just a trifle insecure.'

'No, Sister, let me finish; what I, I "said" was a dying huzzah of . . . what I no longer believe. You were – are – right.'

My projected self looks at my brother's projected self. 'About?'

'About old dogs, new tricks, not-so-splendid isolation from la Voie Ombragée; and about . . . a higher purpose. Will that do for now?'

Well, this is a U-turn: 'Have I wandered into an orison?'

'If you're going to gloat, Sister, you can bloody well—'

'No. I'm not gloating, Jonah. I've been waiting thirty years to hear you say this. We'll go to Mount Shiranui. The west of Japan is heaven in the autumn. Enomoto Sensei wants to meet you. She suggested a dozen ways to improve our operandi.'

The projected Jonah contemplates an ending and a beginning. 'Good. Okay. That's decided, then.'

I think of my brother and me as foetuses sharing Nellie Grayer's womb, one hundred and sixteen years ago; and of our birth-bodies, sharing our lacuna for eight decades. Strangers are 'They', a lover is first a 'You' and then a 'We', but Jonah is one half of 'I'. I focus on the matter at hand before I say anything sentimental. 'Your throat will hurt like holy hell when I pull the hairpin out, but I'll cauterise the wound and—'

'Now or never, Sister.' Jonah puts his left forefinger on our guest's frontal chakra eye. With his right hand, he glyphs her awake . . .

. . . and Iris Marinus-Fenby's pupils dilate in the orison's uncertain light. 'Stay still, Iris,' says Jonah. 'You've been in an accident, but everything's fine. You're in hospital. You're safe.'

She's as feeble and scared as she sounds: 'Accident?'

'Black ice on the M4 side of town. Your VW's a write-off, but nobody else was involved, and your injuries don't appear to be that serious. You've been here all day. You're in the Royal Berkshire Hospital.'

Marinus swallows and looks dazed. 'I . . . Who . . . ?'

'Yes, I'm Gareth Bell, and this is Dr Hayes. All quacks together. Iris, to help with your treatment programme, we'd like to ask a few diagnostics – are you up to it, do you think?'

'Oh . . .' the Woozy Shrink squints, 'yeah . . . sure. Go for it.'

I take over: 'Thanks, Iris, that's great. Firstly, can you tell us if you're in any pain right now?'

Marinus checks she can move her hands, then her feet. 'No, I . . . I . . . just numbness, I guess. My joints ache a little.'

'Uh-huh,' I scribble on my clipboard. 'The IV's feeding you anti-inflammatories and painkillers. You sustained some nasty bruising up your left side. Secondly . . . limb mobility, you just did that for us, great – who said that doctors make the worst patients?'

'Well, hey, maybe psychiatrists make better ones.'

I smile. 'Great, I'll tick my "tribal affiliation" box.'

'Do I have any breakages?' asks Marinus, trying to sit up.

'Whoa, whoa,' says Jonah-as-Dr Bell, 'Iris, take it *easy*. The neck brace is just a precaution, don't worry. We haven't X-rayed you on the off-chance that you're pregnant. Might you be?'

'No. Definitely not pregnant.'

'Great,' I say, 'we'll take you up to X-ray in an hour or so. Vision: how many fingers?' I hold up four.

'Four,' says Marinus.

'And now?' I ask.

'None,' says Marinus.

'No problem there,' says Jonah, 'though we're a tad anxious about concussion – there's a doozy of a contusion round the back of your noggin. We'll CAT-scan you after your trip to X-ray, but what recollections do you have of the accident?'

'Uh . . .' Marinus looks haggard and worried. 'Uh . . .'

We sit down on her bed. 'You recall being in your car?'

'Yes, but . . . I remember arriving at my destination.'

'O-*kay*,' Jonah says. 'Where was this destination?'

'A passageway, an alley, off Westwood Road, on the edge of town. Slade Alley. I'd gone to meet Bombadil.'

'"Bombadil"?' says Jonah. 'Not the Green Man leprechauny one from *The Lord of the Rings*? What a bizarre alias.'

'Uh . . . I – I – I never read it, but my Bombadil's a conspiracy theorist. I don't know if that's his real name or not. He's a research subject. I'm writing a paper on abduction fantasies. He was . . . in an alley, and . . . there was a door in a wall that wasn't normally there . . .'

'Fascinating,' I say, looking a little alarmed. 'But I *promise* you, Iris, the only place you've been today is the Royal Berkshire Hospital.'

'You know better than us,' Jonah says cheerfully, 'the

tricks a mind'll play on itself after a trauma or accident. But look, you've told us what we need. If you'd just take this paracetamol to staunch any minor internal bleeding you may have sustained' – Jonah flips up the bed's swivel table and places the pill on a little white dish – 'I'll text Viv Singh at Dawkins to say you're conscious and verbal. They've been on tenterhooks all day.'

'Yes, thanks, I, uh . . .' Marinus gazes at the easy-to-swallow pill.

My evoked heart in my evoked body beats a little faster.

I look back. Jonah puts a glass of Evian water by the dish.

'Thank you.' Still bleary, Marinus picks up the pill.

I look away. *Swallow it*, I think. *Swallow it whole.*

'No worries,' says Jonah, unworriedly, as if our metalives aren't dependent on this fickle woman doing as he bids her. Jonah scrolls down his contacts, mumbling, 'Viv Singh . . .'

'Uh . . . could I just ask a question?' asks Marinus.

'Fire away,' says Jonah, not taking his eyes off his iPhone.

'Why in the eleven thousand and eleven names of God would I oblige two parasitic soul-slayers by imbibing their poison?'

The wall-clock stops; the LEDs on the monitors die; a far-off telephone falls silent; and Jonah freezes, with his back to both me and Marinus. I stand and back away, stumbling and sick. My brain insists that Marinus, a guest, cannot know more about us than Jonah and I know about her; that a mortal psychiatrist cannot be lying in an evoked bed in our inner orison, watching us calmly like a committee member at a dull meeting; and yet she does, she can be, she is. 'Of all the shortcomings in your oper-andi,' our guest is saying, 'your "banjax" is the most anti-quated. Truly! An anima-abortifacient so fragile that unless the patient imbibes it of his or her *own conscious volition* it fails to work – we haven't seen the Shaded Way deploy such a primitive formula for fifty or sixty years. What were you thinking, Grayers? If you'd only updated it you could have injected it into my body just now. Or tried to, anyway.'

Sister, Jonah telegrams, *what is she?*

Danger, I telegram back. *Change. A fight. An ending.*

Kill her, Jonah urges. *Kill her. Now. Both of us.*

If we kill her we lose her soul, I telegram my uncensored thoughts, *and if we lose her soul, our operandi dies – it won't last nine more hours, let alone another nine years. And if the operandi dies, there's no more lacuna.*

'And without the lacuna,' Marinus says out loud, 'the world's time floods in, shrivels up your birth-bodies, and then your soul's off to the Dusk, right? One hundred and sixteen years: over and out.'

Jonah's appalled face reflects my own; he telegrams, *Can this trespassing bitch hear us, Sister?*

Marinus tuts. 'Mr Grayer! Shoddy abuse. "Bitch" is a stingless insult these days – it hurts like, I don't know, a celery-stabbing. And "trespassing"? You invited me here today to get my soul sucked out – and for accepting your invitation I'm now a trespasser? Not nice.' With a casual glyph, Marinus revokes the IV drip and neck brace. We can't conceal our astonishment. 'Yes, I know about sub-orisons in orisons, a bubble in a bubble, the attic in the house. It's not a bad copy; but *Evian* water? In an NHS hospital? Don't tell me – that was *his* genius idea, wasn't it?' The intruder looks at me but nods towards my brother. I don't answer. Unhurriedly, she gets out of bed and Jonah and I both take a step back. 'You'd know better than to conjure up fancy French mineral water, Miss Grayer, after your top secret undercover stake-out at Dawkins Hospital. I saw you, studying me through Viv Singh's eyeballs. I reeled you in, as you reeled me in. A company of reelers. Classy pyjamas, but,' she glyphs and her own clothes reappear, 'I'm a creature of sartorial habit.'

Jonah has let the sub-orison half fade to conserve voltage, which is wise. A brute-force attack on Marinus, however, which I fear Jonah is planning, would be less wise. I sense she's expecting it.

'You have us at a disadvantage,' I say. 'You are?'

'I am who I am, Miss Grayer. Born Iris Fenby, 1980, in Baltimore; "Marinus" got added later, hereditary reasons, long story; my family moved to Toronto; I studied psychiatry; and here we are.'

I probe. 'But you're telepathic; you glyph . . . Know what this is?' I float a gentle psychowave her way, which she deflects at the Evian bottle. It tips over, trundles to the edge of the table-top, but vanishes before falling off. 'Look at that, Jonah,' I say. 'Our guest and we are three peas in a psychosoteric pod.'

Marinus is not amused. 'Leave me out of your pod, Miss Grayer. I don't use human beings like disposable gloves. Did you even thank that poor wretch Mark – "Bombadil" – before tossing him into the garbage just now?'

'What a lofty hill of divine compassion you sit on,' I needle, I speculate, 'to care for every one of humanity's mewling, puking, rutting seven billion.'

'Ah, you people always say that,' the intruder tells me.

'Do we?' I say. 'And how do you know our names?'

'Therein hangs an hour's tale.' Marinus takes a gadget from her jacket and shows us. I see the word SONY. 'One of you, at least, has seen this digital recorder before, and I'm guessing it was *Mr* Grayer . . .' She turns to Jonah, who peers closer. 'Yes. See if this jogs your memory.' Marinus presses PLAY and we hear a woman's confident voice: 'Interview with Mr Fred Pink at The Fox and Hounds pub, Saturday, twenty-eighth October, 2006, 7.20 p.m.' It's Freya Timms. Marinus presses STOP. It's no great feat to read our faces. 'She had a life,' says Marinus. 'A sister she loved.' Her anger is controlled but fierce. 'Go on. Name her. Or are you too ashamed?'

Jonah looks too appalled to name anyone. So the fool should be. His bragging Self-as-Fred Pink nine years ago, as he toyed with Freya Timms in my orison of The Fox and Hounds, spun this Ariadne's thread that led Marinus to the heart of our operandi. And when my brother regains the power of speech he spends it on the wrong question: 'How did you get that?'

Marinus stares back him and looks at me.

I meet her gaze with no shame at all. 'Freya Timms.'

Marinus stares back, then peers through the half-gone blinds over the ghostly windows. 'Dark nights, in these parts. We're in your attic at Slade House, right?' I don't answer. The intruder returns to Jonah's question. 'Your "crematorium" disposes of bodies well enough, but inorganic matter falls through the cracks. In the old days it hardly mattered – a button here, a hair-clip there, but in this century' – Marinus turns back to us and weighs the recorder in the palm of her hand – 'angels really do fit onto pinheads, and the lives of the multitudes inside a memory stick. We are few, Miss Grayer, but we're well connected. Artefacts like this,' she drops the recorder into her pocket, 'have a habit of finding us, sooner or later.'

I'm forming a theory. Enomoto Sensei spoke about 'vigilantes' with a pathological urge to slay fellow Atemporals.

'Who *is* this "us"?' Jonah demands of the intruder.

'Why not ask your sister for her view? She gets out more.'

I keep my eyes on Marinus. 'She's from across the Schism.'

'Warm.'

'Le Courant Profond,' I guess. 'The Deep Stream.'

Her hands are free to glyph. 'Warmer.'

What a stupid guessing game. 'You're an Horologist.'

'Oh, say it with more venom. Spit out the vile word.'

Marinus, like Jonah, has a taste for burlesque irony. Like Jonah, she may trip.

Jonah, naturally, hasn't heard of Horology with a capital *H*: 'She makes clocks?'

Marinus's laugh sounds genuine. 'Miss Grayer, I almost understand why you tolerate this plodding clerk, this risible thesp, this dim corgi who fancies himself a wolf. But come: between you and me, is he not a liability? A ball and chain? An aptly named Jonah? Did your Sayyid never tell you what he thought of him? "A preening fool composed of a pig's afterbirth." His words, I swear. We hunted your former master down in the Atlas Mountains, with the aid of Freya's recording. So we must thank your brother for that much, at least. The venerable Sayyid begged for mercy. He tried to buy it by telling us more than we had hoped to learn. We showed him the same mercy he'd shown *his* prey down the decades. No more, no less. And now Jonah has proven to you what a lethal encumbrance he is—'

She breaks off, having brought my simmering brother up to boiling point: Jonah is glyphing up a pyroblast with his bare hands. I telegram *Don't!* but Jonah's head is roaring and he can't hear so I shout it out loud – 'Don't!' – as the vestiges of the hospital room fall away, revealing the long attic of Slade House. Eighty years of metalife end at this forking path: do I join Jonah's assault against an untested enemy who has goaded us to attack her? Even if our victory would end in voltaic starvation? Or do I forsake Jonah, watch him fry, but keep alive a foetal hope of survival? Even as Jonah rashly, rashly, applies every last volt in his soul to Marinus's incineration, I don't know what to do . . .

. . . Marinus, fast as thought, glyphed a concave mirrorfield; it quivered under impact, I heard the crackle of lava and saw Marinus's face snap with pain, and for a moment I dared hope that our intruder had underestimated us; but the mirrorfield held, regained its flat plane and flung back the refocused black light straight at its source. There was no time to glyph or warn or intervene – Jonah Grayer lived for over 42,000 days, but he died in a fractured second, killed by a beginner's trick, albeit a trick deployed by a master. I glimpsed a carbonised Jonah with melted lips and cheeks, trying in vain to protect his eyes; saw him wither into split briquettes and grainy cinders; and watched a nebula of soot lose its human form and fall to the floorboards, smothering a constant candle.

My decision had made itself.

I see the glow of the candle through my own birth-eyelids. I hear the faintest wheeze and crackle of beeswax, boiling in its pond at the wick's stem. Time, then, has bled into the lacuna. Our operandi is dead. When I open my eyes, instead of Jonah opening his eyes, I will see Grief. Grief and I exchanged words in Ely many years ago after Mother died, poor wretch, coughing her lungs up, telling me to take care of Jonah, to protect him, because I was the sensible one . . . And for over a century I honoured that promise, and protected my brother more assiduously than poor Nellie Grayer meant or dreamed, and during these years Grief was only a face in a crowd. Now, however, Grief intends to make up for lost time. I'm under no illusions. Jonah's soul is gone to the Dusk: his birth-body is an ankle-high soot drift around my feet and the base of the Ninevite Candle. The pain Grief intends to inflict will be colossal. Yet, curiously, for now, just for now, I find myself sitting in the dead wreckage of our operandi, amongst the grainy remnants of my twin brother, able to consider my position with a calm clarity. Perhaps this calm is the silty stillness between the sucked-away sea and the tsunami's roaring, horizon-wide, hill-high arrival, but while it lasts, I'll use it. I let Jonah die his futile death alone – proving, I suppose, that my love of survival is stronger than my love for Jonah. Survival is also an ally against Grief: if I buckle now, I won't survive. The killer is here, in our attic. Where else would she be? I heard her a little while ago. She picked herself up, gasped with pain – good – and creaked across the old oak boards towards the candle flame like a monstrous, hobbling moth. She's waiting for me to open my eyes and begin the next round. I'll keep her waiting a little longer.

Dark skin in the dark space, she watches me watch her, a hunter watching her cornered quarry, our optic nerves connecting our souls. Jonah's murderer, Marinus the

Horologist, who brought death into our stronghold. Yes, I hate her; but how far short it falls, this petty, neutered verb. Hatred is a thing one hosts: the lust I feel to harm, maim, wreck and kill this woman is less an emotion I hold than what I am now become. 'I was expecting you,' she speaks in a funereal hush, 'to join your brother's assault. As, doubtless, was he. Why didn't you?'

The end begins. 'Because it was an abysmal strategy.' My throat, as usual, is dry as I reinhabit my own body. 'If we lost, we'd –' I look at the soot on my feet '– end up like this.' I stand – my joints are stiff – and take a few steps back, so the candle is equidistant between Marinus and me. 'Yet if we won, we'd die when the lacuna collapses and the world's time catches up with our bodies. Typical of Jonah. Even when we were children he would act rashly, and leave me to sift through the wreckage and somehow make things right. This time, I can't.'

Marinus considers this. 'I'm sorry for your loss.'

'Your condolences disgust me,' I say, mildly enough.

'Grief hurts, yes. Every human you ever fed on had loved ones who suffer now as you do. Without even a figure to blame, to hate. But you know the proverb, Miss Grayer: "Who lives by the sword—"'

'Don't quote proverbs. Why didn't you kill me just now?'

Marinus makes an *It's complicated* face. 'First, cold-blooded murder isn't the Deep Stream's way.'

'No, you prefer to goad your enemies into shooting first, so you get to plead self-defence.'

The hypocrite doesn't deny it. 'Second, I wanted to ask you if you'd kindly open this inner aperture –' she indicates the tall mirror '– and let me out.'

So she's neither all-doing nor all-knowing. I don't tell her that even I can't open the aperture now the operandi is dead. I don't even confirm that the aperture is the mirror, in case she's merely guessing. I just think of Marinus dying when the air in the attic runs out. A satisfying image. I tell her, 'Never.'

'It was a long shot,' Marinus admits, 'but it would have been more elegant than Plan B, which is also a long shot.' She steps towards the candle and reaches into a thigh pocket. I marshal my voltage for a defence. Instead of a weapon, however, she produces a smartphone.

'The nearest network is sixty years in the future,' I tell her, 'and the aperture won't relay phone signals to the real world. So sorry.'

Her dark face glows in the smartphone's cold light. 'Like I said, it's a long shot.' She points her device at the aperture; stares; waits; checks the screen; frowns; waits; waits; steps around the candle and the soot drift to crouch by the aperture and examine the surface of the mirror; waits; presses her ear against it; waits; and finally gives up with a sigh. 'Too long a shot, it would appear.' She puts away her smartphone. 'I stashed half a kilo of plastic explosive in the shrubbery, by the outer aperture, when you-as-Bombadil weren't looking. My canvas bag. You felt something was amiss as we walked beneath the wisteria,

I believe, so I distracted you. I hoped the explosion would blow open this aperture from the other side, but either the phone signal didn't reach the detonator or your operandi is too solidly built.'

'I'm sorry for your loss,' I enjoy saying. 'Might there be a Plan C, or is Dr Iris Marinus-Fenby going to die today?'

'Traditionally, we'd stage another climactic battle between good and evil. We'd never agree which of us is which, however, and the only prize on offer is a slower death by oxygen starvation. Shall we forgo tradition?'

This false levity is repugnant. 'Death for you is just a short break, I understand.'

She steps back, around the candle, and sits where our guests are — were — usually positioned, opposite the aperture. 'It's more troublesome than that, but we do come back, yes. Was Enomoto or the Sayyid your principal informant on the Deep Stream?'

'Both. Both masters knew of you. Why?'

'I met Enomoto's grandfather in a former life. A murderous demon of a man. You would have liked him.'

'You deny us the privileges *you* enjoy.' My voice sounds chipped and cracked. It's this thirst.

'You murder *for* immortality,' states Marinus. 'We are sentenced *to* it.'

'"Sentenced," you say? As if you'd willingly swap your metalife for a bone clock's snatched, wasted, tawdry handful of decades!' I feel unaccountably tired. Suppressing my grief over Jonah's murder must be wearing me out. I sit down, a foot or so back from my usual place. 'Why do you Horologists conduct this . . . this . . .' the word's gone, it's Arabic, it's used in English these days, too, 'this . . . jihad, against us?'

'We serve the sanctity of life, Miss Grayer. Not our own lives, but other people's. The knowledge that those future innocents whom you would have killed to fuel your addiction to longevity – people as guiltless as the Timms sisters, as Gordon Edmonds, as the Bishops – will now survive: that's our higher purpose. What's a metalife without a mission? It's mere feeding.'

What Bishops? 'All we did' – my voice sounds too wavery – 'was seek survival. No more than any sane, healthy, animal—'

'No,' Marinus scrunches up her face, '*please*, no. I've heard it so often. "Humanity is hardwired for survival"; "Might is Right is nature's way"; "We only harvest a few". Again and again, down the years, same old same old . . .'

Pain is growing in my hips and knees, a pain I've never known. I wonder if Marinus is responsible. Where's Jonah got to?

'. . . from such an array of vultures,' the woman's saying, and I wish she'd speak up, 'from feudal lords to slave traders to oligarchs to neocons to predators like you. All of you strangle your consciences, and ethically you strike yourselves dumb.'

The pain has spread to my left wrist. I examine it and if I could, I'd drop it, horrified. My skin is sagging like a grotesque, ill-fitting sleeve. My palm, my fingers are . . . *old*.

A repulsive illusion, surely, of Marinus's creation. I peer forward – with unseemly effort – to look into the aperture. A white-haired witch stares back, aghast.

'The explosion didn't smash the aperture,' says the black woman, 'but it did make a crack. Across the middle, there. See?' She crouches next to me and runs her finger along a thick line. 'There. The world's leaking in, Miss Grayer. I'm sorry. You're ageing at, perhaps, a decade every fifteen seconds.'

She's speaking English, but what's she talking about? 'Who *are* you?'

The woman stares at me. Which is very rude. Don't Africans teach their children manners? 'I am Mercy, Miss Grayer.'

'Well then, Mercy – get me . . . Get me . . .' I know his name, I know I know his name, but his name doesn't know me. 'My brother. This instant. He'll sort it all out.'

'I'm sorry,' says Mercy. 'Your mind's decaying.' She rises to her feet and picks up our . . . what's it called? The thing the candle sits in? She's going to steal it! 'Put that back!' I try to stop her, but my feet just twitch uselessly in a pile of dirt. This place is filthy. Where's the housekeeper? Why is this African holding up our candlestick? That's the word: candlestick! We've had it in the family for generations. It's three thousand years old. It's older than Jesus. It's from Nineveh. I call out, 'Bring me Jonah this instant!'

The African lifts it up, like a, like a, you know, like a thing . . . and swings its heavy base into the mirror.

★

Daylight floods and snowflakes swarm through the splintered plane of the aperture, covering the floorboards, scurrying around the darkest recesses of the attic, like inquisitive schoolchildren. My body has shrivelled up around me like a punctured and bony balloon. Untied, unzipped, unstrapped from its senility-riddled brain, my soul floats free. Marinus, without a backwards glance, steps through the aperture even as the attic fades away into a wintry sky, above an anonymous town. It's over. Without its birth-body anchoring it to the world, the soul of Norah Grayer is dissolving; momentarily it hovers in the mid-air space once occupied by the attic of Slade House. Was that my life? Was that all? There was supposed to be more. Many, many decades more. My cunning had earned it. Look below: roofs, cars, other lives, and a woman putting on a green beret, leaving the scene via an alley, with a stolen candlestick still in her hand. There is no farewell in the busy air, no hymn, no message. Only snow, snow, snow and the inexorable pull of the Dusk.

Not yet. Not *yet*. Dusk pulls, but damn the Dusk, damn Marinus, I'll pull harder. *She killed my brother and now she's walking free.* Let Grief pull with me; let hatred strengthen my sinews. My stock of seconds may be meagre but if there's a way to avenge hot-headed Jonah, my precious twin, my truest other half, I'll find that way, however faint the traces. Brick chimneys; slate roofs; thin, narrow gardens with sheds, kennels and compost heaps. Where might a vengeful soul find refuge? A new birth-body?

Who can I see? A brother and sister, at play in the snow . . . They're old, they're already too interwoven with their own souls. Another boy jumps on a trampoline . . . he's even older, of no use. A magpie lands on a garden shed with a crawk and a tinny thump but a human soul cannot inhabit an animal's brain; a garden away, a back door opens, and a woman in a woollen hat steps out holding a bowl of peelings. 'No snowballing your sister, Adib! Build a snowman! Something gentle!' She's pregnant – it shows, even from thirty feet up, and now I see it all. I see the beauty of the pattern. The woman is not here by chance: her appearance is caused by the Script. Dusk hauls me to itself, but now I perceive an alternative fate, I resist. My newborn mission makes me strong, and my mission is this: one day, however distant, I will whisper into Marinus's ear, 'You killed my brother Jonah Grayer – and I kill you now and for all time.' I transverse down with the ponderous snow, the living snow, the eternal snow; undetected, I pass through the mother's coat, her underclothes, her skin, her uterus wall; and I'm home again, my new, warm home, my anchorage; immune to the Dusk and safe in the brain of a foetal boy, this miniature, drowsing, curled-up, dreaming, thumb-sucking astronaut.

ACKNOWLEDGEMENTS

Maximillian Arambulo, Nikki Barrow, Manuel Berri, Kate Brunt, Amber Burlinson, Evan Camfield, Gina Centrello, Kate Childs, Catherine Cho, Madeleine Clark, Louise Dennys, Walter Donohue, Deborah Dwyer, David Ebershoff, Richard Elman, Lottie Fyfe, Jonny Geller, Lucy Hale, Sophie Harris, Kate Icely, Kazuo Ishiguro, Susan Kamil, Trish Kerr, Jessica Killingley, Martin Kingston, Jacqui Lewis, Alice Lutyens, Sally Marvin, Katie McGowan, Caitlin McKenna, Peter Mendelsund, Janet Montefiore, Nicole Morano, Neal Murren, Jeff Nishinaka, Lawrence Norfolk, Alasdair Oliver, Laura Oliver, Lidewijde Paris, Doug Stewart, Simon M. Sullivan, Carole Welch. Sincere apologies to anyone I've overlooked.

Thanks as ever to my family.

THE BONE CLOCKS

David Mitchell

National Bestseller
Longlisted for the Man Booker Prize 2014

Run away, one drowsy summer's afternoon, with
Holly Sykes: wayward teenager, broken-hearted rebel
and unwitting pawn in a titanic, hidden conflict.

Over six decades, the consequences of a moment's
impulse unfold, drawing an ordinary woman into
a world far beyond her imagining. And as life in
the near future turns perilous, the pledge she made
to a stranger may become the key to her family's
survival . . .

'Chock full of twists that create the sensation of
reading six books coiled up in one, this enthralling novel
is a dazzling display of Mitchell's virtuoso abilities.' *Chatelaine*

'Thrillingly entertaining.' Zsuzsi Gartner, *National Post*

'Fantastical, ambitious, bold and exuberant.' *The Observer*

'Mitchell is funny, hip and full of life . . . a beautiful
explosion of adventurous ideas.' *The Times*

'Combines fantastic inventiveness with depth and heart.'
Justine Jordan, *Guardian* Books of the Year

Vintage Canada
www.penguinrandomhouse.ca